Daniel's CD

M. P. REYES

Second paperback edition September 2020

Book cover design by 100Covers.com

ISBN 978-1-7352362-2-3 (paperback)
ISBN 978-1-7352362-3-0 (ebook)

FOR MY PARENTS who supported me. For my brother who calmed me down that one night when I finally said that I'll send this story out to the world. For my sister who listened to my ideas. For my love who inspired me and wanted to know what happened next in all my stories. And for the man who I never got to meet.

This one is for all of you.

Author's Note

FOR MY ISLAND readers back home and all over the world,

As you read on, I am sure that you will notice the lack of Chamorro words in this novel. One of my intentions before even writing this story was to bring familiarity of the culture to the world, specifically through our dying language. But as I went on writing, I found the rituals and actions of our close-knit families and friends are what reveals us more than just our language.

I also realize that you may find similarities in the words, phrases, and names of the characters and events in this book with people you may know in real life. However, this whole story truly is fiction. It is a product of imagination and is one of the many stories that I am sure countless others have formed in our culture.

Please read on. I hope it sparks something in you.

M. P. Reyes

"Restore then, O conscript fathers, life to him from whom you have taken it. For the life of the dead consists in the recollection cherished of them by the living."

— Marcus Tullius Cicero, *Philippicae*

Prologue

I HAD A thing for the sky, especially today with its layers of pink, orange, and blue streaking upward and out from the sinking sun.

I stood behind the front screen door of my home in Sinajana, watching the sky with music playing in my head. Or was it playing on a stereo somewhere? I couldn't tell. But it didn't matter since my focus was on the sky and the many stories under its watch. To people who think nothing of it, the sky does nothing but tell time and look pretty, and that is true. But to me, the sky is also the ultimate witness of stories.

"Nice day today, huh?" a familiar voice said. I turned to see a face I hadn't seen in a while, not since his burial five years ago. My dad's. But somehow, instead of shock at seeing my deceased father, I felt calm, like it was any typical day. As if my dad had never left.

I stepped out and pulled up a chair beside him. He had an opened beer in his hand as he breathed in and out, stretching and smiling. Healthy.

"Yeah, it's beautiful," I answered. My dad handed me a beer as the sun continued to sink.

"How's your day, son?" he asked me, like he always did when he was alive.

"It's good. It's great actually. Mia's mom is going crazy with the wedding planning, and it's driving her crazy. But she calmed down. And we all had a good rehearsal night."

"Yeah? Your brothers were there?"

"Of course. I wouldn't get married without them there."

"Good."

I opened my beer can, but found myself staring at it, wondering if I should even drink it. I don't like beer. A special occasion was the only thing worth putting in the effort to tolerate that bitter taste. And this didn't feel like a special occasion—just any other day when he was alive. But something was telling me to drink, and it wasn't peer pressure.

The bottom of chair legs scraping against the concrete floor of the garage sounded. Once I looked up, I saw Uncle Dun sitting next to Dad, grabbing a beer from the small cooler between them.

"Big Man," Uncle Dun greeted me.

"Uncle Dun," I said back, smiling before I bowed my head to amen him, the usual greeting of the young ones to the elders of the Chamorros. He pinched my nose and I yanked back, laughing before my eyes flitted to the sun disappearing in the sky. For one second, I appreciated it. The next had me wishing that I had more time with Dad after the last sunrise we'd watched together.

I shook off the thoughts when I realized I was wasting time sulking about something I couldn't change.

"You in love, son?" Dad asked me, breaking me out from my thoughts.

It was a question I hadn't expected to hear him ever ask. But it was also a question that triggered a grin on my face that I couldn't shake away if I tried.

"I am. You would have liked her."

"He knows. He's been watching over you and your brothers like a crazy man," Uncle Dun said. Dad rolled his eyes and hit him in the chest. But he turned back to me, our eyes meeting. "She's a good one, son. I'm glad you found her."

He held his beer can up for a toast and cheered, "Here's to Veo and Mia!"

"Thanks, Dad," I said before toasting him. I tipped my can to hit Dad's then Uncle Dun's and took a long sip of beer. As I did, I heard the words Dad used as a farewell, a good-bye without ever saying good-bye. And once I heard it, I didn't have enough time to blink.

I woke up to the sound of the alarm. For a second, I found myself feeling light and content. But once my realization kicked in, the feeling disappeared. It was all in my mind.

A dream, I thought. *It was all a dream.*

"AHH MAN! I love this song! *And I'll love you! I'll love you when the full moon's out!*" my younger brother Matthew sang. He continued singing as Dominic, my other little brother, fixed my tuxedo by the large mirror. Matthew was a year younger than I was, and Dominic was the baby, two years younger than me.

Streaks of sunlight beamed through the windows that were poorly covered by the sheer, white curtains that danced as the breeze blew in. The melodies of the island song sounded from outside. It must be blasting where the speakers were since this room was the farthest from the wedding site.

"Whenever I hear this song, I think of Kayla, man. Our first date. I took her out to eat. Then we slow danced on the beach under the moonlight," Matthew said. He swept the room with his arms as if he were dancing with his partner.

"He drank a few already," said Dominic.

"Yeah, I figured," I chuckled, watching Matthew spin around in the air.

"Is this you guys' song too?" Matthew asked me as Dominic turned me to fix the back of my tux.

I shook my head and told him, "No. This song is too sappy."

"Ahh. . . it's funny how songs can trigger memories, huh?" Matthew said. The idea flew past my head with thoughts on how anyone could like this song.

"Trigger memories?" Dominic asked.

"Like how when I hear this song, I think of Kayla even though she isn't here yet. She isn't in this room. I don't see her here, and yet I think of her because I heard a song that we danced to before."

He had already lost Dominic's attention. I could tell by the rolling of his eyes as he continued patting me down. It felt like forever to fix a tux.

But a song. A memory. A simple tune to bring back a moment in the past. "Huh. You're right," I said. "Sometimes, those memories don't even have the songs playing. It was a moment we somehow assigned a song to."

Matthew squinted, raising a brow. The classic look of confusion.

"Like," I tried to bring up the best explanation I could think of. "You can associate a time in your life with a song even if that song wasn't playing in that moment."

I could tell that I was losing him fast. "A sad song can make you think of a sad moment, like a break-up. Even if you never listened to it while you were trying to get over the girl."

"Oh, because of the lyrics," Matthew tried to reason it out. But everyone usually paid attention to the lyrics of a song. Growing up, I saw how people regarded the voice of a song as the major role of music. Not the tunes or notes or rhythm. Those were seen as background noises to the voice, but I knew better.

"It can also be because of the organization of the sounds."

Matthew shrugged it off and plopped himself down on the couch in front of the TV where we had been playing video games for the past two hours. It was official. I'd lost him.

I turned to Dominic, hoping that he caught the last bits of the conversation so I could talk about it more. But the busy look on his face already said that he hadn't been listening the whole time.

I cocked my head back, rolling my eyes at the ceiling. *Ai Adai*. But it was okay. I'd just tell Mia when I got the chance.

Dominic finally finished fixing my tux.

I sat down beside Matthew who had his hands on a controller, playing *Mortal Kombat 11*. I would have played with him, but as soon as I sat down, my mind raced off to other things. I stared at the screen, but my attention was elsewhere. I wasn't nervous like people told me I'd be. This "cold feet" crap didn't work on me. I loved Mia. We both thought of weddings as this unnecessarily big celebration of love. But it was an unnecessarily big celebration of love that she wanted her dad to be a part of. And with his memory deteriorating, it had to be now. Mia would regret not having a wedding if it was only her mom walking her down the aisle.

I felt good about it, avoiding a regret, but something else was bothering me. Did I forget something? I considered the possibilities as I sorted through everything I could think of. But then I remembered last night's dream. I hadn't forgotten anything or anyone. It just felt incomplete because Dad and Uncle Dun were invited. They just couldn't come.

A squeak came from the direction of the door. It was Mom, standing in the doorway. She was a simple woman. She didn't dress up for many events, but she'd dressed up for today. Before anything came out of my mouth, my arms were already around her, locking her in an embrace. "Thanks for coming, Mom."

"Of course, my Veo. I wouldn't miss it for bingo night."

My chest felt heavy as I struggled to free her, but eventually, I did. She placed her hands on my cheeks with that proud mom smile. "Oh, my boy! You are getting married!"

I chuckled. "Yeah. I guess I am."

"And here you are. The least likely to get married among your brothers, because you didn't like all that serious stuff. Maybe you'll change your mind about kids and actually have one."

Again, I chuckled. Having kids was a topic for another day, so it wasn't worth discussing now.

"Well! I just wanted to see you before I sat down," she said as she turned for the door. But then she spun back around to face me as she searched through her purse. "Oh! I almost forgot. I brought you something." She pulled out something small and flat—a CD inside a white paper casing. Looking through the opening, I saw someone's handwriting on the top.

"Daniel's CD," I read.

"It's so you don't forget who is also here today," Mom said with a glowing face that triggered my own smile.

I hadn't forgotten.

Changing the subject, Mom pointed out how much she was looking forward to the crab at the reception. She giggled. "And now, my boys, I'm going to find a seat."

I told her to enjoy the day as she left, leaving a pleasant aura in the room. It was going to be a good day.

"That's Mom," I muttered. The smile on my face wouldn't go away—it was because she was a part of this day. That was one of the effects of losing a parent. I started thinking of life without the other one like it was going to happen tomorrow, if not today. Today of all days though, I couldn't be more grateful that she was here.

"What did Mom give you?" Dominic asked. Matthew jumped off the couch and grabbed the CD, which I snatched back fast.

"A CD?" Matthew asked when I pulled it out of the paper casing. I checked for scratches.

"Dad's CD," Dominic said once he read Dad's handwriting on the top.

I scanned the room, finding an old stereo beside the large mirror Dominic and I had been standing in front of. I plugged it in to find that it still worked and put the disc on as my brothers stood in place. As the CD disappeared into the stereo, I realized what we were about to do.

The first song began playing, a tune I knew our dad loved. As it continued to play, so did my memories, locked into each song.

TRACK #1
Love Between the Sheets

When I was 8 years old. . .

UNCLE DUN ASKED me something in the middle of a party. "Do you know what our last name means, Little Man?" All eyes turned to me.

"Mafnas?" I asked.

"Yeah. That's your last name, isn't it?"

"I don't know." Every one of my relatives laughed at me. "I mean, I don't know what it means!" I corrected myself.

At that point, everyone was still laughing, nodding. The conversation went on to other topics as if I wasn't going to get an answer until Dad turned to me.

"When you walk along the beach, there are footprints you leave in the sand."

"Is that what it means? Footprints?"

"The shore comes up and down. And when it comes up, you know you won't find your footprints there when the shore goes down anymore."

My eyes fell to the ground.

"That's our name," Dad said.

It wasn't like I dreamed of being famous like everyone else seemed to. My brothers and Dad were all I cared about. I only needed us, the Mafnas Men and the Man, to take on adventures. My mom was the one who coined that name for us: the Mafnas Men. But she never referred to Dad as "the Man." That was something I came up with since he was always in the picture, unlike her. He'd be that navigator in a submarine or the pilot in a plane. And my brothers and I would be the divers, studying and swimming with the fish. Or we'd be the gunmen, shooting at enemy vehicles.

I wasn't always with them, because of our parents' separation. At the time, I didn't know why my parents separated. The night they decided on splitting, they sat us down and told us that Mom would be moving back to Saipan with only me. She said that it was because she had to take care of my grandma, but to take only me didn't make sense. And why she sent me back to live with my brothers and Dad a year later, I also didn't know at the time. I thought she got tired of us and only settled for me but then couldn't even handle that.

I still had my brothers and my dad though. There was one summer day when Dad called us in for lunch and we came in from playing and dreaming. We were sweating and out of breath, but Matthew told Dad that we were going to climb Mt. Everest one day. There was another day where Dominic told Dad that we were going to jump out of a flying airplane. It'd be the three of us forming a circle in the sky as we fall through the clouds. People on the ground that we'd expect to look like ants would be wondering, "What's that in the sky? The Mafnas Men? They're crazy!" Another day, I was the one to tell him that we'd each be a stuntman for an awesome action trilogy in the future. Of course, he asked, "Why not be the stars?" But we all knew we didn't want that. We just wanted to be the epic workers of a great story that needed to be told.

"Like *Star Wars*!" sang Matthew.

"Or *The Lord of the Rings*!" I said, since I wasn't a big fan of *Star Wars*. But our footprints would not be washed off or erased like our last name meant. Long after we are gone, people would remember us.

Uncle Dun's booming laugh snapped me back to the present. I was slouching on my chair in the middle of the family gathering. But the moon and stars were out. My brothers were bored out of their minds as Dad laughed with our aunts, uncles, and everyone older than us by a large scale. Then our Auntie Connie busted out her new karaoke machine. This wasn't one of the adventures I expected to remember years later, but I do. It was a part of the song that Auntie Connie would sing, and it was all because it ruined my mojo later in the night.

At the time, streetlights weren't everywhere. But because I lived next door, I knew the area well. I wasn't scared of the dark, not even in the jungle. I only had one fear, and that fear wasn't going to surface anytime soon, which brought on a great idea of mine.

"Hey!" I whispered to my brothers. "Hide and seek! You in?"

"Yeah! Let's go!" said Dominic, his face lit with excitement. According to Matthew, that excited face had been coming on a lot since I moved back.

We ran out into the dark after Dad asked where we were going.

"Hide and seek!" Matthew answered before disappearing into the dark.

"Okay," Dad waved. "Be careful, boys."

It started off with us three for the first two rounds. But
soon, our cousins were in the dark, hiding while someone
was seeking. It wasn't difficult to avoid being the seeker, or
the "It" as we liked to call the role. Like Matthew, I was
fast. I evaded so many touches with ease that I knew that
if I became "It," it would only last for one round. As I hid,
I thought about this theory. Was it true or was I thinking
too highly of my skills?

Get caught, I told myself. *See for yourself, Veo.*

John, my ten-year-old cousin, was the seeker. He wasn't
the fastest or the fittest. He was actually one of the slowest,
and when I let him catch me, the teasing began.

"A-ha! I can't believe you got caught like that!" Matthew
said. Our other cousins joined in, even as I told them that
he only caught me because I heard something in the jungle.
But nobody was listening. The teasing kept on. I could
only squint, waiting for the opportunity to prove them all
wrong and to prove my theory right. So I tolerated the
teasing for a couple more minutes before I turned around.
I leaned on my forearms on the base and counted down to
my transformation as the epic seeker. The epic It.

I began counting from 20. A song ended on the karaoke
machine, leaving only adult conversations in the distance.
Near silence, the darkness of the night, and an epic seeker
to beat the many who teased him.

"3. . . 2. . . 1. . ." I counted as loud as I could. But
once I turned around to play the game that I was to beat,
the lamest song to ever play came on. It was a song that

belonged to a hotel ad where a couple booked a night only to laugh and roll around in the white sheets. Sappy. I growled before I heard some snickering in the dark. I pulled myself together and finally announced, "Ready or not, here I come!"

When I blended in the darkness, I tried to feel my eyes turn red or silver. I wanted to see the glow in my eyes as the hiders would see it. I knew they were watching. I soon had evidence as I saw a pair of eyes looking at me from behind a metal trash can. The bright lights from the family gathering shining behind it made it the worst place to hide. I ran to the metal trash can and reached it before the eyes appeared over it again. I caught him. It was Dominic, the one who had reflexes of a crab. He tried running for the base, but my hands already had a grip on his shirt. He had nowhere to run, and I knew everyone would agree that he was the next It.

I threw my head back, roaring with laughter, at the thought that the first person I saw, I caught. I was so good. I was so fast. Nobody could beat me, especially Dominic. My hands still had a grip on his shirt when he shot a frustrated look back at me. "Let go of me!"

"You're the next It!" I sang with my hands still gripping his shirt.

"Let go!" he said as he pulled away from me before stomping back to the base. All the other kids had run to the base and were laughing at him, telling him the same thing I did. Dominic pouted with crossed arms until one of the other kids said something I didn't pick up on. He laughed, listening to her as he looked at me. I could tell they were talking about me, but at that point, I only had a story of the quick seeker that was me. The only thing wrong with the story was the karaoke song that was still playing on the machine.

It's been too long, yeah
I wanna hold you in my arms
Keep you tight within my hold
Until we hit our world
For tonight, would you mind keeping
Our love between the sheets

I saw Dominic laugh again before counting with no warning that he was starting the next round. But John stopped him once he saw his sister, Valerie, coming down the steps. "Mind if Val joins?" he asked.

"Not at all! The more, the merrier," Matthew said.

"Can I count now?" Dominic asked before John gave him a thumbs-up. Dominic began counting, sending a rush through everyone to hide.

My pulse raced as I scanned the area. Everyone was going to the areas that I usually hid in. Dominic was almost finished counting by the time I actually ran for a hiding spot. The spot behind Auntie Connie's unused grill.

He won't find me here, I thought.

Finally, he turned around, looking around for any movement. There were no sounds but the music coming from the gathering, and it wasn't my sappy seeker song anymore.

I tried to stop my breathing. I felt it was the loudest. His line of view studied my area before taking a step my way. But a cough in the opposite direction took hold of Dominic's legs and he ran in another direction. There was my chance to reach the base. I got up and reached it in a second. I was so fast, and this was confirmation. Other kids joined me, touching the base. I laughed out loud, "A-ha! Dominic didn't catch me!"

All the other kids joined me in this laughing session. We watched Matthew, the only one Dominic found, evade his touch. And soon, Matthew made it to the base, joining in on the laughing at Dominic who was going to remain the seeker for the rest of the time we played. "Ha-ha! Dom's too slow!" the other kids laughed.

Dad came down, changing our laughter to discussions or silences. "Come on, boys. We're going home. You got school tomorrow."

Without saying goodbye to the other kids, we started for home. I heard Val's voice vibrate in my ear as she yelled "Good night! See you tomorrow!"

When I turned around, I saw her grinning as she sat on John's shoulders. John had no trouble carrying her. A big brother. Big. I should be able to do that, carry one of my brothers. But even if I could carry them, having them sitting on my shoulders didn't look right. I figured that maybe that was a Val and John thing as I waved back, walking only a house away.

Dad was so far ahead when I turned back toward our place. He probably needed to use the toilet. But my brothers and I kept our pace since we knew where to walk to avoid trees and rocks and the little garden that was invisible in the night. We knew our place well.

"Ha-ha!" I laughed. My energy was still so high as I

skipped around with Matthew following my movements. Words were spilling out of my mouth before my mind caught up with what I was saying.

"Can't catch me right now!" I taunted Dominic. "Sloth!" I called him.

Of course, Matthew didn't know what a sloth was, but he joined in anyway. Dominic didn't respond. But by the time we got through the front screen door, Dominic picked himself up with his stature as tall as it could be. He was calm as if our words didn't affect him. My child brain told me that I was wasting energy teasing someone who was as sturdy as a rock. For a second, I admired my little brother. I kept admiring him until he walked into the bathroom that had thin walls. And through these walls, I heard him squeal on me with the most elegance I've ever heard in his voice. "Dad, I don't mean to be a tattletale, but I think you should know. Veo has been bullying me."

Matthew silently laughed at me, mocking as he pointed his finger at me. All I could hear was the toilet flushing.

"Is he in trouble?" Dominic asked. He was pulling up all my anger to place it between the prongs of a slingshot that would soon hurl toward him.

"Yes, he is," Dad answered before telling Dominic that he'd handle me when he was done on the toilet. Dominic walked out of the bathroom with a smirk that belonged to the most villainous of cartoons. With his gaze directed at me, he strode through the kitchen to the living room, I knew he was telling me to brace myself for Dad's wrath. I pulled everything in me together to not break the competitive stare, but my anger got the best of me after two seconds.

"You tattletale! You're such a snitch!" I pushed him, and soon he was fighting back. He slapped me, making my cheek sting. As I pulled my fist back, he pushed me as hard as he could, yelling, "You Saipanese! You don't know how to fight! You're all talk!"

"HEY!" Dad stepped in, breaking us apart with just his hands.

"Veo, get your pillow and blanket now. You're sleeping in the living room tonight," he said with his voice as deep as I ever heard, successfully scaring me.

Dominic tried to say that I had hit him first, but he only interrupted, "It doesn't matter! I don't want to know! Don't ever hold that 'Saipanese' crap against someone. You have family there. You and Veo are brothers. No more fighting."

"But Dad! He hit—"

"No! Quiet! It doesn't matter. Go to your room! Veo, out here, tonight. I don't want to hear it."

Dominic stomped his way to the room and closed the door behind him. Dad shot Matthew a look that pushed him off to bed without a single word. I froze standing in place while he tried to rub the frustration off his face. "*Aii*," he started. "Get the belt, son."

"Dad, but I didn't—"

"GET THE BELT. I'm not going to say it again."

I took one of his belts that sat on his dresser in his bedroom and handed it to him. It wasn't the first time I'd gotten spanked. I had gotten spanked so many times that I knew to brace myself the second before the belt stung my skin. But that night, I was angry. It wasn't enough hearing the belt whip Dominic from the living room either. I still

17

went to sleep with angry thoughts about the little snitch in the house.

By ART CLASS in school the next day, I was still upset with Dominic. Before we had even left for school, he came to the breakfast table with giggles and smiles from the wonderful night's sleep he had. He looked at me with a wide grin on his face. I could feel him mocking me. I knew he was thinking it. *Oh, look at me. I had my beauty sleep in the air-conditioned room while my bully of a brother slept out in the hot living room that needs to be aired out by the windows that stink of both stray dog and chicken poop.*

"Good morning, Veo," he greeted me with a smile that only communicated ridicule.

I stared at him, hoping he'd feel my death glare focused on him and only him. But a smack to the back of my head reset my face's emotions. "Stop it. Eat," Dad ordered. Matthew shook his head, chuckling once Dad disappeared into the restroom.

"Grudges aren't worth having if they waste your time. And they almost always do," he said, sounding wise. But I ignored it. He was acting like a smartass, giving advice that he knew nothing about.

Since then, my head had been boiling with thoughts that emanated from knowing that Dominic was laughing at me. Even from different classrooms, his laughter vibrated in my head, infuriating me. The fuel in me was in reserve for recess. Dad wouldn't be around. And with my fast moves, I could show Dominic who was boss before any teacher could ever reach us. It was the perfect time.

The bell rang and Mrs. Johnson called everyone into the line for lunch. Everyone in my class grabbed their lunch bags before we headed out the door in a single file. Once I was out that door, I felt it, my stomach gurgling from hunger. All the focus was on my stomach now as it made noises that I hoped nobody heard. What made it worse was knowing that our classroom was the farthest from the cafeteria. I chanted the tune I heard army guys cry when they walked to move my attention away from my stomach. *Left. Left. Left. Right. Left. . .*

Once we were out on the field, I found another distraction. I felt the tingles on my skin, the kind that usually told me that I had been in a cold room for too long. I felt like I was glittering in the sun even though I knew I looked like a popsicle with clothes and hair walking through a grassy field. But it didn't matter. The tingles felt good.

We soon made it to the cafeteria. My classmates and I sat at our designated table before we began munching on what we had packed. I usually didn't pay attention to where Mrs. Johnson went. The cafeteria was a kid's world. Not an adult's.

I opened my lunch bag to find my favorite food: sausage and rice wrapped in foil and a warm apple. I forgot everything I had planned to do as I started eating. I heard my classmates talking but paid no attention to it as I usually did. I just felt the joy of eating and kept to myself.

As I finished up, a loud burst of laughter came from the long table next to my class. It was Dominic's class getting up. I was cleaning my things when a chunk of his class formed a small circle. It looked like they were gathering around something or someone. I tried to look at what was happening, but I couldn't see sitting down. I got up and made my way through the group to find them laughing at someone. I moved around people to find that it was Dominic, who was laying on the ground, holding his stomach with groans and tears that told me someone had punched him. I scanned the area quickly and took notice of a chubby boy who threw his head back laughing. Two other boys were patting his shoulders, cackling as they joined in the crowd. The chubby boy looked down at my little brother and pulled his leg back for a kick. In a moment, I had him on his back on the ground. I threw two more punches before pulling back.

The crowd went quiet as I hooked my brother's arm over my shoulder, helping him get up. I carried him away from the crowd, intent on bringing him to the restroom to clean him up. We almost made it past the doors of the cafeteria when Mr. Nolan and Mrs. Johnson stopped us, separating me and Dominic.

"No!" I yelled. "He's my brother! He needs my help!"

"Mr. Nolan is bringing him to the school nurse. You, Veo, are coming with me to the principal's office."

I NEVER LIKED Mrs. Johnson. She was a boring teacher. I always got in trouble for leaving my desk to stretch when I was falling asleep during her lessons. She didn't know how to entertain, and she didn't know how to play any fun games. She only ever gave the class 30 minutes of playtime, which was ridiculous! She even thought I was dumb for not saying anything to anyone. And now, here she was, having me sit with her in front of the principal's office, waiting for Dad.

"What you did was wrong, Veo," she said whenever I opened my mouth. "Now, quiet."

My angry eyes shot daggers at the ground. I knew the floor couldn't feel anything, but if it could, it would be scared by how mad I was. Even I would have been scared if I could have seen myself glare at the ground.

The bell over the door rang as Dad came in. The office lady pointed to Mrs. Johnson, who was already standing with her hand out. Dad shook it as he greeted her. "So what needs my presence today?" he asked.

"We appreciate you coming in today. But our principal would like to address the situation with you himself."

Dad lifted a brow at me. I might as well be his troubled child with the ongoing problems I kept giving him. I knew a deafening lecture from him was coming. "Of course, Mrs. Johnson. When can we see him?"

Before she could answer, the principal opened his door and welcomed him in. "Come on, Veo," Dad called. I followed as I looked back at Mrs. Johnson who turned around and headed out the door. I groaned, sticking my tongue out at her, but she was already long gone. She couldn't sense me disliking her from this far away.

We took our seats in front of the principal's desk. "Mr. Miller, is it?" Dad began.

"Yes. Yes. Mr. Mafnas, do you know why you and your son are here today?"

Dad shook his head. "Mrs. Johnson said you'd prefer to tell me why."

"Your son here was in a fight." I felt Dad's gaze turn on me. His stare was heavy enough that I could already hear the screaming that was to happen an hour from now at home.

"A fight. . ." he repeated.

"He punched a kid several times for hitting your other son, Dominic." Dad's stare was still heavy, but it shifted back to Mr. Miller. I glanced at him, hoping that the reason made a difference, but his face was expressionless. I couldn't tell what he was thinking.

"Here, in school, we handle things diplomatically, Veo. We do not resort to violence. Not now, not ever. We can always solve things with our words," said Mr. Miller, addressing me now.

Dad agreed with him as he furrowed his eyebrows at me. The heat of his anger was warming up before he addressed the principal. "I appreciate you calling this to my attention, Mr. Miller. Rest assured that I will deal with my son at home."

The conversation went on between the two before Dad and I left for the nurse's office to pick up Dominic. Once we did, we headed to the car with Dominic's arm over my shoulder again. The same way I would have helped him an hour ago, before adults stepped in and stopped me.

THE CAR RIDE was quiet. All I heard were the gears shifting and the wind blowing through the rolled-down windows. I was sitting in the front passenger's seat with Dominic in the back. I didn't know what to say, so I stayed silent.

This was one of the times when I questioned who was wrong and who was right. I remember people in church telling me that violence was wrong. Throwing people's things around was wrong. Hitting someone else was wrong. Flipping other people's tables was wrong. But I remember a story of Jesus flipping over merchants' tables, scolding them about how this was the Lord's Temple. And maybe he was right. But if Jesus was the ultimate example of how to react to things, then physical violence was one way to solve a problem. I mean, he flipped people's tables around before saying anything. Right?

The answer to that Jesus story was something adults told me I'd understand when I got older. But they always said that. I didn't care for that type of answer. I still tried to find the true reason with my childish mind.

As for this situation, I found myself staring at Dad as he drove. I still couldn't tell what he was thinking, if he was upset with me or not. Fear was building up.

But with time whipping past us, making me more and more impatient for an answer, I opened my mouth. "Dad?"

"Yeah?"

"Are you mad?"

His face was still expressionless. He didn't look mad, or frustrated, or happy. He looked calm, as if his thoughts were on something else, even as I reminded him of my fight.

"I'm not, son."

The silence filled the car again. I thought he'd say something more, but he didn't.

"Am I in trouble?"

Dad stayed quiet until he pulled up in front of EZ-PZ Mart. I didn't actually notice we were heading in this direction until we parked. He turned to me and started, "What do I always say, Veo?"

I thought about it for a second and guessed, "'Stop playing and eat'?"

He shook his head.

"'Get down from the roof'?"

"No. What do I always say about your brothers to you? You, especially, since you're the oldest."

"'Always look out for your brothers'?"

"Always look out for your brothers, Veo. You're being a good brother if you're protecting them. Always protect them."

"But what about what Mr. Miller said?"

"Mr. Miller is wrong. He doesn't know how to be a good brother."

"But he's an adult."

"Adults can be wrong, son. Rely on what you think you should do and if you think it's right. If you think those adults are bullying Dominic or Matthew, punch them in the face, and I'll be there with you in prison."

I couldn't help the smile coming on. It was a nice thing to hear, but did he mean it? Once I got the look on Dad's face, I knew he did.

Dominic grinned as he leaned up on the center console with an attitude that said all the problems from the day disappeared. "What if you're the adult who is doing bad to us?"

"Then Veo, Dominic, protect each other from me. Even from me. Always protect each other. Punch me in the face too, and I'll smile in prison knowing that you did the right thing."

We all joined in laughter followed by ice cream that Dad treated us to. The rest of that day was calm and happy. But his words echoed in my mind all throughout the day and the years that followed. The duty bestowed upon me by my birthright, which I happily accepted.

Even from me. Always look out for your brothers. Always protect them.

TRACK #2
Follow the Road

When I was 20 years old. . .

I SAW THE difference in the rain in Seattle and the rain on Guam. I couldn't escape noticing the difference as I walked home. The sky was light gray with no hint of the sun. The light was masked by the clouds. The raindrops fell, unappreciated for the little beauty they held, unlike the raindrops back home that would have most likely landed on something green, like the leaves of the mango tree outside my home.

In my mind, I could see the raindrops tracing the leaves before landing on the ground. Sometimes they'd be tracing the mangos that were ready to drop, accompanied by some sunlight that knew where to shine to make it look like the most vivid of paintings. It was something I took for granted, expecting that the sun knew where to shine everywhere in the world, but today, I realized it didn't. The sunlight didn't know where to shine here.

I took a deep breath, nearing home. The gray sky on this day only had me recap what happened so far.

"This is unacceptable. This is the worst service I've ever had!" I heard the customer yelling at work. I continued making his taco after glancing at the long line behind the angry man. The pressure was on, but I kept telling myself to calm down. I didn't work best when I let the stress get to me, I knew that much.

The company phone rang, successfully adding the perfect amount of noise that completely drowned the only thing that was keeping me sane at this job: the music. I sighed, deciding if I should answer it. But after a couple of seconds, the ringing became such a nuisance as it vibrated in my aching head. "Tacos Tonight. This is Veo speaking."

The angry customer seemed to have gotten louder. Fortunately for me, I could only listen to two people at a time.

"Veo, there's a long line. Where are the other two?" my manager asked from the other end.

"I'm the only one working, sir."

"You're the only one? Where's Lori and Frank?"

At that point, I could only tell him that I didn't know. It wasn't my job to know. It was his.

"Why didn't you tell me about this earlier?"

"I did, sir. I texted you and called about two hours ago. You said you were going to call them."

A long pause from the other end told me that he wasn't listening when I told him hours ago. All that came out on the other end was "I see. Just finish the line," then a dial tone.

"Okay, boss," I muttered before turning to find that many customers had grown impatient and left. I couldn't say that I blamed them. But that wasn't my fault. A chuckle came out of me as I cursed under my breath. Today felt exhausting.

"You realize that your slow pace has killed off half of this line, right? And now you're laughing?"

I shook my head before giving him his order with my mouth still curved. The customer was cranky. And based on his appearance with the ill-fitted suit that looked too tight on his thighs but too big on his gut, I could only speculate that he was on a diet. And given that his order was two tacos and a bottle of water, it was a diet that was going to fail very soon.

The look on his face when he saw his food on the tray was bittersweet. His eyes weren't satisfied, but they were grateful that there was finally food within reach. He said nothing as he took the tray and walked away.

As for me, I had no idea why I was smiling. Perhaps it was my realization on how screwed I was from seeing how long the line could get, and how I had to attend to it alone because two co-workers didn't show up. They didn't even call. And my manager didn't even do anything about it. So to hell with it. If everyone in this company couldn't bother caring to avoid this happening, then I shouldn't either.

I returned to the prepping table to cut up more lettuce with my back turned to the customers. *Customers came first! Blah, blah, blah.* I knew that customers came first, but with the lettuce cut up, it'd be faster to bring them their order.

"Hey, can I get some service here?" a voice behind me said. It sounded familiar, but I didn't entertain it.

"I'll be right with you," was all I said.

"No, I demand help now!" This was accompanied with a suppressed giggle, but I ignored it.

"Sir, please take my order," the voice said with a tone of finality. I clenched my jaw, trying to rid myself of all the frustration that was building up again. But deep breaths in and out had helped me in the past as they did now before I turned around. To my surprise, I found a friend I hadn't seen since high school ended two years ago.

"Seung! What the heck!" I stopped cutting, holding my hand out for him to pull me in for a hug over the counter. "When did you get here?" I asked, noticing his build hadn't changed. He was still soft and of average height that hadn't changed since high school. He usually dressed neat, but today he was wearing pajama pants with a jacket over a black shirt and running shoes.

"Stopover. I'm leaving back to California tonight."

"Aw man. Well, it's good to see you, my friend." I kept on smiling as my attention returned to the line behind him, which was almost nonexistent. There was only one customer other than Seung. They all must have lost faith in getting their lunches before their breaks ended.

"Did you want anything, man?"

"Just a good birthday for you," he answered. "Happy birthday, Veo."

Pulling my hands together, I brought in my inner girl out as I sang, "Aww, shucks, Seung. You're so sweet!"

The one customer behind him left the store as Seung rolled his eyes, laughing at me. "And to get an answer on why you're still here."

I could only raise a brow as I said, "Because I have to work to make money for my rent and food and—"

"No. You know what I mean." My eyebrows met, surprised at the question. It wasn't something he normally asked. Our conversations were made up of stories of what was going on, not advice or deeper questions like he was asking now. I wanted to know why he was asking, but the time stood out in my mind. I didn't want to waste this time with questions I could ask in a chatroom.

"It's a good place, man. How are Jason and Ding? Are they still in California?" I asked only to have Seung shake his head, chuckling.

"You always had a way with changing the subject. But you won't escape it this time. Why are you still here?"

"Why? What's wrong with staying here?"

"Based on what you tell me, dude, you're lonely here."

"No, man, I have Hannah. I'm fine."

Seung lifted a brow at me. "You sound like my ex-girlfriend whenever I asked if she was alright."

"Hey, come on. I'm good here. It's a good place to make money."

"Right."

Changing the topic, I asked him how the flights were and how it was from wherever he was traveling from. How long until he graduated from college too.

He entertained the topics, reminding me of high school all over again. Then he touched on how dirty the restaurant looked from over the counter. I told him how I often found myself staring at the health ratings post on the front that rated it "Excellent!" wondering if the department was rigged and biased, because there was no way that fruit flies (or whatever species of flies they were) in the kitchen would get an excellent rating.

"Sounds gross," Seung said with a twisted face. His eyes

scanned the area behind me before they shot me a look, asking me if I was sure I still wanted to stay in Seattle.

I'd moved here after high school with the hope that a variety of possibilities would have my blood pumping faster. There were things that I could do here that I couldn't do on Guam. I could go ice skating. I could get good coffee to warm myself up like they did in the movies. I'd have a long list of museums, parks, hiking trails, bars, restaurants, and all that stuff to get to on a day off. There were so many things to do here, and I was going to get to it.

But the problem was that there was winter. Once I opened the door, a near icy breeze blew against my face that sent chills to every inch of my legs, slowing my whole body down. It made me take a lot longer than I should have. The cold made everything too uncomfortable. Summer and spring were easy, but winter was too damn long.

Now though, wasn't a time I wanted to talk about it, because I didn't want to admit it. I didn't know if I had any more hope for my stay here. But I knew I didn't want to move back home, because there were some things that weren't worth my attention. Some things I wanted to escape. Matthew was the only brother back home anyway.

As for the other states that I could move to, well, I didn't want to admit that Seattle was a bust. I had been told that it was a great place to live, and for the whole time that I had been here, I had been waiting for that title to kick in.

I didn't know how to respond to a look, so I glanced back at the clock and studied the area for tasks I was putting off. I wanted to end the conversation, but I also didn't. Seung caught on quickly though. "Well, Veo, you know how to reach me if you want to stay with me and the guys in Cali."

"I know. Thanks, man," I said, making an effort to pull a grateful smile together before he asked his last question.

"So how's that gorgeous girlfriend of yours?"

It rang in my head as I made it to the steps of my apartment building. I was done for the day, and the response of a normal person would be to escape under the sheets. But I stood before the entrance of the apartment, staring at a doorknob, wondering if I should even go in. I could go to the store and get more things to cook for a good dinner. Or maybe I could sit on the steps here and do nothing. My legs were numb, or at least, my brain was making them feel artificially numb for the moment so I wouldn't have to go in. And it worked. I turned around and planted myself on the dry stairwell that stood nearby.

Usually, I didn't care much for my birthday. I only wanted a good day. I'd requested today off, but unfortunately, my manager paid no mind to my request.

Happy birthday to me.

But even if I got a day off from my job, I wouldn't know what to do or who to spend it with. I had Hannah, but she'd beg me to join her in the nail salon. She wasn't that expensive of a girlfriend, but she was always begging me to get a pedicure since men did it now. It was fine if other men did it, but I didn't feel comfortable with people massaging and picking at my feet.

I took a deep breath, remembering my brothers. The last time I had seen both of them was at the airport when I left for Seattle. We were full of jokes then. They had yet to finish high school, so they couldn't follow me. And even when the opportunity presented itself, they chose what they chose. Matthew: to stay on Guam with Kayla because (and I'm sure he'd deny this being the reason) she couldn't get into the schools he got accepted to. And Dominic: to Indiana on a scholarship to the same college Matthew turned down the year before. It sounded like they both were doing well, but I wished they were around.

The sky was cloudy today. Out of those clouds came my curiosity about how it would be to jump from an airplane and form that circle Dominic was talking about when we were kids. That circle that would destroy whatever clouds were in our dropping paths. Us. The Mafnas brothers.

I didn't think I'd be living this kind of life. Where I followed the motions of life and work. Wake up. Breakfast. Work. Come home. Dinner. Entertain myself and the girlfriend for a couple of hours. Sleep. Then repeat it all over again. If I kept this up, my grave would be another stone on top of a dead body that had not really lived in a casket buried under soil. That was a fear of mine: to not be a part of anything that mattered.

I took a deep breath until I heard her voice behind me. "Babe?"

My heart dropped, feeling stress begin in my forehead. "Yeah?" I asked.

"What are you doing?"

"Just taking a break."

"A break from what? Our place is upstairs. But you know what? I need your help with something. Follow me." Hannah went down the stairs and disappeared around the side of the building.

I stayed sitting for a few more seconds, trying to enjoy

myself, until she called after me again. "Veo! Come here! Come on!"

I took another deep breath as I rolled my eyes and got up. As I got in her car, she asked me if I had my ID.

"Yeah. Why?"

"Good. Because we're going to the nail salon. They'll give us a discount for your birthday."

I groaned, rubbing my face. "I'm sorry, babe, but I really want to rest."

"Come on. You'll like it," she said as she checked her face in the mirror.

"I really don't think I would."

She shot me a look. An argument was under way if I didn't agree with her, so I threw my hands up in defeat.

"Sorry. Let's go." But by then, Hannah's mood was set to one that would trigger a fight with the next wrong thing I said.

Crap.

I SAT DOWN in front of my desk, blowing out my frustrations of the day. I wasn't expecting it to be the best day ever for my birthday, but at least, again, I wanted it to be a good one. But life wasn't like that.

At her command, I drove after we finished at the nail salon. She didn't say why she didn't want to drive. Maybe because of her new fragile nails that were already dry but couldn't handle a steering wheel. But it didn't matter. I drove anyway.

"Oh, can we stop at that new Chinese restaurant? We can eat there for your birthday dinner."

I didn't fight it again. We had a good dinner, kind of. The place was crowded. Our orders took an hour to reach our table, and another fifteen minutes to give me my correct order. But the waitress was friendly. I wasn't going to give her a hard time, like Hannah was.

After the meal was taken care of, the bill came. Immediately, Hannah told me to handle the bill.

"Not that I don't mind paying, but isn't it my birthday?"

"But I paid for the nail salon. You have enough money in the bank."

At that point, I didn't say anything. I could have questioned how she knew what was in my bank account, but that would only cause a fight. Hannah had argued with me in public quite a few times. I drew a breath in to keep my sanity.

"Right," I muttered, forgetting that she had ears of an owl.

"You showed it to me, remember?" She dropped her hands and glared at me. "We both agreed that we'd share our finances too, so I have to see it anyway."

"Yeah, yeah, yeah."

I placed my card in the little slot of the black folder and handed it to the waitress, who smiled at me. "Thank you, sir," she said in a friendly tone.

I thought nothing of it, but in the corner of my eye, I saw and heard Hannah clicking her jaw.

"What?"

"Nothing," she said, but something was clearly bothering her. I didn't want to ask again. But that backfired later in the night. By the time we got home, we were fighting over the look the waitress gave me and how I should expect to pay since I was the guy in the relationship. Of course, I didn't fight much. It was mostly her ranting over and over again, louder each time I opened my mouth.

"You never listen to me! We talked about sharing our money, getting a joint bank account, and—"

"So why did I have to pay if we're shar—"

"Because you're the man here, Veo! *You take the bill.* It doesn't look right if I take it even if we're sharing."

I felt defeated. There was no rationale in what she was saying.

I slumped down my desk chair. Hannah had fallen asleep, crying. *Great,* I mouthed. I threw my hands in the air in defeat and let gravity pull them down. Whatever. It was just a day.

I turned on my laptop, about to scroll through social media. But before I could scroll, a notification popped up. Seung had sent me a link to a video hours ago. One click opened a slideshow of landscape photos that might as well be default desktop wallpapers. My ears were graced with Seung's poorly sung alteration of "Follow the Road" as audio.

Follow the road
To the unknown
California, San Francisco
Follow the road

I laughed at the end of the video as Seung appeared. Before he said the one thing that settled a decision that

I didn't think I was entertaining, he clicked his tongue, winked, and pointed to the camera. He was a friend I was missing from miles away.

"We're waiting for you, bro," he said.

He was a friend who lived with my other friends. I could live with them in a week if I tried. I thought of the things I would be giving up here, but that didn't last long. The only thing I'd be giving up was Hannah. Hannah for California.

Hannah. Seattle. Rain. California. Matthew. Dominic. Seung. Jason. Ding. Happy. Dad. Phone. Advice. Ringing.

I must have dozed off because my phone's vibration woke me up as I drooled on the desk. My eyes felt heavy as I tried to read the name of the person calling me at 3:39 a.m. It was my dad.

"Hello?"

"Veo?"

"Yeah. Yeah," I said sleepily. "It's me, Dad."

"Sorry, boy. What time is it there?"

"Oh, don't worry about it. How are you?"

"I'm good, son. Really, if it's too early over there, I'll call—"

"No. No, it's okay. I actually want to ask you something."

He waited. I thought the line had cut, so I asked if he was still there. He was always as quiet as a cat. Their smooth movements as they jumped on counters without a sound, that was like him with breathing. He was a smoker, and still incredibly silent.

"I'm still here. What is it?" he asked.

"I might be moving to California."

Again, silence. At that point, I remembered that

Dominic and I planned to visit him over the summer. It was a plan we made last year that never surfaced, because we never talked about it afterward.

"I won't be able to visit you and Matthew if I do," I continued, "because I only have enough for a one-way."

Again, silence. My heart wasn't pounding fast, but it was pounding. I didn't even know why. I didn't look up to him. I didn't owe him anything. He was part of the problem back home if he wasn't the whole. He wouldn't know much about moving off Guam anyway, since he couldn't do it for Mom.

"I see," he started. "Well, it's okay. Let me know what's going on. Is Hannah going with you?"

"Uh. . .maybe."

I didn't expect it, but I heard him laugh. "Okay. But keep me in the know."

There was some small detail to the way he was saying things. I didn't know what it was. He sounded sad, or perhaps he sounded like he was hiding something, but I couldn't tell. Usually when he hid something, he didn't talk. But it was hard to not say anything on the phone and keep a conversation going.

"I will, Dad," I finally said.

"Take care of yourself," he said.

"You too, Dad."

The line cut off.

"So how's your dad?" Hannah asked at the breakfast table. She was eating something with a whole lot of green in it for this meal, so I didn't touch it. I grabbed the cereal and milk instead.

"He's alright. Why?" I asked as I took a few bites.

"Heard you talking to him last night."

I nodded, avoiding eye contact with her. I was still feeling some weird sense from her about last night's fight. From what I'd learned over the course of our relationship, I knew I should never talk about our past fights. Always wait for her to forget about them. "Mhm."

Silence. Still the awkward vibe hung in the air. But I finished my cereal. As I reached for my bag that sat on the chair behind me, I said, "Well, time for work."

"Babe?" she asked as I was about to reach for the doorknob.

"Yeah?"

"When were you going to tell me that you were moving to California?"

My head was buzzing with a headache by evening since it was being bashed in with Hannah's repetitive statements. She'd said these things before, but fifty times more today about how she knows I always just sit in front of her, pretending to listen to her, and how she knows that I never take what she says seriously because I start slouching and my eyes grow weary. To be fair, that's all because we usually fight in our poorly lit apartment. That starts up another fight. I never appreciate the things she does for our living space, and worse, to her, I do nothing for our apartment. I know that wasn't true, but once I open my mouth, she's already on how I always argue with her instead of listening to her, how my mouth is always bracing itself for the next thing to say against whatever she's saying, especially about girls she knows are flirting with me. I'm subconsciously flirting back, according to her, because I'm a guy who thinks with the head on his dick and not his actual head. This always triggers me to help her feel less insecure about our relationship, but it ultimately fails, because she ends up with the same thing she says about us all the time even though it contradicts many arguments she uses against me: that we don't talk anymore.

My mouth hung open as I felt the pulse in my head beat harder. I had missed a whole day's worth of work, but all I could think about was getting away from the source of this headache.

Oh, dear God. If you exist, give me strength.

I managed to stand up and walk for the bedroom. "Where are you going?" Hannah asked.

"To bed."

"Oh, you're not going to California? Hey! I'm asking you! You're not going—"

"I was, and now I'm not. I was going to surprise you." I started lying, anything to get me out of this situation. "I was going to ask you to move with me to California, but apparently, you're not taking the idea too well, so forget it!"

I looked at her, my eyes tired. For a second, she looked regretful, but she fought it, still trying to pin the blame on me. "You should have told me sooner if that was the case!"

I spun in the direction of the bedroom, ignoring her, which must have stunned her, because she said, "Geez, I'm sorry. I didn't know."

She repeated what she was saying and tried to grab my arm, but I waved her grip off, acting like the situation bothered me.

"Veo! Crap. I'm sorry."

"Whatever."

"Let's do it. Let's move," she said. Her eyes grew wide with hope, but I knew that even if I were to move to California, I couldn't imagine her being there, so I told her the truth. Well, the half-truth.

"I don't know, Hannah. It might not be right for you."

"Nonono. It is. It is," she insisted, planting kisses on me.

"But what if—"

She kept kissing me, shutting me up. I tried to get the words out of my mouth, but she kept shoving them back in me. She pushed me into the bedroom and onto the bed, kissing me. I felt tired, too tired to even get water, but Hannah was doing all the work. And I was too tired to say no to her tonight.

JUDGING BY THE hint of light reflecting off the mirror from the slits of the blinds covering the window, it was safe to assume it was the next day. I'd slept heavily. That was the upside of difficult nights, the sleep afterward felt like Heaven.

I looked behind me, finding Hannah's beautiful eyes still shut, asleep. She was a shapely woman with a light skin tone. She was out of my league. In the beginning, I didn't even think to try, but once I managed to get her laughing, we started talking more and more. Believe it or not, she was a good friend of mine, but I suppose the sexual tension ruined it all. What's done is done.

I took a deep breath as I stared at the ceiling, wondering about California. It wasn't even an option before Seung came around, but now, I wondered if I would be happy there. Because happiness was all that mattered, right? Would I be happy there with Hannah? We used to be close friends, and maybe I *was* a crappy boyfriend, but I could always change that. I could tell her where I go and when I go. I could tell her who I'm with, and I'd only hang out with my guy friends. It wouldn't be so bad, and I'd have Seung around to help me out.

Hannah groaned as she moved slowly. She rubbed my chest with her eyes still closed, and said in a low voice, "I love you, Veo."

I intertwined my fingers with hers as the corner of my lips rose. "Let's do it," I whispered. "Off to California." I saw her smile, but she went right back to sleep.

Off to California, we go, I thought. *To California. With Hannah.*

A vibration went off somewhere. It kept going. A call. I followed the sound to my pants that were on the floor at the foot of the bed and saw the caller was Matthew.

"Hello?" I whispered as I left the room, closing the door behind me.

"Veo?"

"Yeah. Hey, Matthew. What's up?"

"What's this thing Dad said about you moving somewhere?"

"Just established it with Hannah. We're moving to California."

"Oh."

"Why?"

"Veo," he started slowly, "I'm sorry, man. But I think you need to come home."

"What? Why?"

"Because Dad's sick." He said the statement that I still hear years later, fresh as if it were happening all over again. "Dad has cancer."

TRACK #3
Queen Marie

When I was 10 years old. . .

MRS. JOHNSON WAS also my third-grade teacher. She didn't change much, so third grade was as boring as first. The highlight of this school year was that I did find out my life's goal. I took some career tests, and I dreamed some crazy dreams. It all made sense for me when I realized it too. I was going to be an astronaut someday! That must have been the only thing I was talking about this year. But hey, I made it through an otherwise boring year. And oh, the last day of third grade was a day to remember.

Usually, I took the school bus back home. But Dad had been out of a job for a while, so he picked me and my brothers up after school for the last couple of months. Even so, it was a surprise to see him in my classroom while my classmates and I finished cleaning up the mess from the end-of-the-school-year party. The air of that day had the celebration of summer sprayed onto it. Once I saw him, third grade was officially over for me. I got my bag and lunch box, heading over as Mrs. Johnson called me.

"So what will you be doing for the summer, Veo?" she asked. I still didn't like her, if I hadn't already made that clear, but I opened my mouth because Dad was right beside me.

"Me and my brothers and Dad are going to Saipan to visit my mom."

"Oh, that sounds so fun!"

"Yeah, we actually might go this summer. Veo here missed his mom last year," Dad said.

"Well, I'm sure that it'll be wonderful."

"What will you be doing, Miss?" I asked, to be polite.

"Me? Oh, I'll be moving back to Minnesota."

"Oh, Minnesota? Why Minnesota?" Dad asked.

"Yeah, why Minnesota?" I chimed in, my curiosity piqued.

"My boys wanted to be with their grandma because she's sick. They moved there last October with my husband, and I've missed them all so much. But my duty as a teacher held me here to wait until the end of the school year. And I'm glad I did, otherwise I wouldn't have made stories with you, Veo, and every one of your classmates. You're just like my son. Such a naughty one, but I can't wait to be with them again."

Dad laughed, continuing the conversation about having naughty sons. They talked more about what being a parent feels like, or whatever it was parents talked about when it came to their children.

But while that was going on, I was getting lost in my own thoughts. I was studying Mrs. Johnson's figure, realizing that she had my mother's body. But unlike my mother, I knew Mrs. Johnson wished to be with her sons.

She was a good parent. She didn't ditch her students, her second set of children, when we relied on her the most. I couldn't help a giggle, thinking that when someone accidentally called her "Mom," it might have made her day.

Even though it was followed by a rupture of laughter, she hadn't been called that in such a long time. It probably did fill some void that was forming in her the longer she stayed here. She just never admitted it.

"Well, Mrs. Johnson, have a safe flight, and I hope your mom gets better," Dad said.

"Thank you, Mr. Mafnas. That means a lot."

Dad smiled at her, one that I knew truly meant he wished her the best. Before we turned for the door, he said, "May our times intertwine again."

All my thoughts were humming the same message—that it was the last time I'd see her. It didn't take long for me to look back at her, waving at a kid that she might never see again. For a moment, I hesitated, but my legs took hold of me, and I ran back to her to give her a hug. After all this time, I'm glad I did.

After I let go of my embrace that could only hug her tummy, I put all my wishes into a smile. I repeated Dad's words as my last ones to her.

"May our times intertwine again."

TECHNICALLY SPEAKING, TOMORROW would have been the first day of summer. But coming home after school on the last day filled me up with so much relief and freedom. I felt it more once I slipped off my shoes and took my socks off, scratching the tight markings they left. For the next few months, I'd get to play with my brothers both here and on Saipan.

"Dad, when are we leaving?" Matthew asked.

"We don't have the tickets yet. I'll get them soon."

"Okay. Don't forget!" he said cheerfully before running into the bedroom to change out of his sweaty clothes.

It seemed like a typical school day, which was still exciting to me since the highlights of my days were after school. But that day was different, and I knew it was once I heard the screen door shake. I turned around to find a furry blonde dog pressing its nose against the metal parts of the screen. My mouth hung open as I turned to Dominic whose eyes lit up at the sight of the beautiful animal.

"Oh, man! What is he doing here?" he said with a grin. We headed for the door as the dog continued to press his nose against the screen.

"Oh, yeah. Boys, this is Buddy. He's our new dog," Dad said.

"What?! He's ours?!" we both said. Matthew chimed in once he came out and registered that we had a new dog. "Where'd you get him, Dad?" Matthew asked.

"Saw him on the street in Tamuning. He was roaming around alone. Got no tags. Had these dirty patches on his fur, so I brought him here. He took his very first shower. Fuzzy one, huh?"

We all agreed. By the looks of his open mouth, panting, and his wagging tail whenever one of us stood up, we could tell he was already a good boy. I would have started baby talking the new addition to our family, but Dominic had beaten me to it. "Ahh! Who wants a tummy rub?" he exclaimed. It ordinarily would have called for teasing, but since I wanted to do it too, I laughed along.

I had lots of plans for what to do with Buddy. I'd play fetch with him like they did in those American movies. Or I'd give him a bath after he rolled around in mud. Or one of these days, I'd take him to Saipan with us. The possibilities were endless.

"Why don't you play outside with him?" Dad suggested as he headed for the dishes. In a flash, my brothers and I were outside, petting him, chasing him, having him chase us. He was a big dog, but I knew he was going to get bigger, especially with our help. I was already thinking about how to groom him and how to keep him in shape. I was so excited to have a dog, too excited, in fact, that I remember tripping over my feet and falling on my face.

Before my brothers could laugh at my expense, Buddy was already by my side, licking my scratched-up face. "Ahh! Buddy! No more kissing!" I laughed and laughed. But it didn't matter, he didn't understand me. He didn't stop licking until Matthew called him over, taunting him to chase after him.

Once Buddy was running again, I turned to face the ocean. But from where I was, the mango tree caught my attention, because Dad was leaning against it, watching us play, enjoying the sight. I wondered why he didn't play with us, but the thought was fleeting, because I saw him point behind me. The moment I turned around, Buddy was licking my face again.

I got to my feet, hearing my brothers discussing the

large pick-up truck tire that sat beside our house. "Let's roll it up the hill!" Matthew said.

"Yeah! Yeah! Get the wheel, Matthew!" I said.

"Me? Why me? I came up with the idea. You guys get it."

Dominic said something as my mind wandered off again. I looked back at the mango tree, but Dad wasn't there. He must have gone inside, I figured. But then, I heard Buddy bark somewhere. I turned to look and saw him running, disappearing into the jungle.

"Buddy!" I called out. I ran after him, and so did my brothers. Soon, we were in the jungle, chasing our new dog. The leaves brushed against our legs and a few cuts were already forming, but I paid no attention to it. I didn't want our dog running away on the first day. I didn't even know what he was chasing.

Just when it felt like he wasn't going to stop, he slowed down. Once my brothers and I made it to him, we were by a cliff overlooking the road. Buddy wasn't chasing anything. But I heard my brothers' amazement at the height. We were right by a cliff with no railings or signs. I felt the need to jump off it. A mini sky-dive. But I wasn't stupid. I could see the cartoon version of me splattering once I hit the ground. My eyes would be blinking, stupidly surprised. I laughed silently to myself as I picked up a pebble and threw it onto the road. By coincidence, a car happened to be driving by. My tossed pebble had missed the car though, and Matthew teased me that I had no aim.

"You couldn't hit a car even if you tried, Matthew," I said.

"Oh yeah?" Matthew challenged. He picked up a

pebble and waited for another car to pass. He threw it onto the road but missed.

"Ha! Told you!" I said as I picked up another. And so began our competition on how many cars we could hit with these tiny pebbles.

I was in the lead with twelve cars, Dominic close by with eleven, and Matthew with nine. We were enjoying ourselves with Buddy close by, watching us. He was our guard dog already, a title I knew nobody else would argue against giving him. He already brought us to our cliff adventure. And now he was sitting by us, making sure that we weren't doing anything reckless. He proved my theory correct when he stood up, barking at Matthew, who was about to throw a rock twice as big as his head at a car.

"Matthew, NO!" I yelled, but I was too late.

The next moments flew by fast. The car brakes slammed after we heard the windshield cracking with great force. Matthew definitely didn't miss this car.

My brothers, Buddy, and I started running for the jungle again. We tried to run away from the problem. Maybe the driver didn't see us. Maybe the driver thought that the rock was from the clouds, that somehow the clouds were angry with them for something they did. I was running on that stupid hope that we wouldn't taste the wrath of a stranger that was old enough to drive. But by the time we made it to our house, the car with the broken windshield was parked in our front lawn. My brothers and I froze as we saw the driver's side car door open.

"MATTHEW! DOMINIC! VEO! GET OUT HERE!" Dad yelled from the living room after I heard the screen door slam. A car engine started outside, and after a few seconds, I could tell the driver was gone. My brothers and I kept to ourselves as we closed the bedroom door behind us. We stood in the living room, waiting for Dad to start lecturing us. It took a while. He kept rubbing his forehead, frustrated. It took such a long while that I couldn't help but notice Buddy outside, looking in. It was like he was waiting for us to play with him again. He didn't know how much trouble we were in. And man, oh, man, did I wish to trade spots with him. To be a dog looking in.

"Sit down," Dad commanded. We did as we were told.

"Dad, Matthew threw the rock," Dominic spilled out softly.

Matthew turned to him, dumbfounded. His eyes darted between him and Dad in a panic. "No, I didn't!"

"Yes, you did," said Dominic.

"No, I didn't! You're such a tattletale! Veo was the one who started it!"

I turned calmly to Matthew on the long couch. At this point, I knew Dad didn't care. All three of us got him into so much trouble that I knew we were all in it together. Matthew and Dominic hadn't caught on yet.

"I don't care," Dad said in a low voice as my brothers kept bickering.

"You're always telling on me, you—"

"You're the one who's always getting yourself into—"

"STOP IT!" Dad yelled. "*Laña*. Boys, because of this, we won't be going to Saipan."

I saw both of my brothers' eyes bulge out before they

started hitting each other. "It's all your fault!" they both screamed at each other, but Dad wasn't having it. His blood was beginning to boil again. He yanked the two away, pushing Matthew to sit in the other chair.

"There. Sit. NOW."

Before Matthew even sat down, Dad began. "Why were you kids throwing rocks at cars anyway? What were you expecting? That they'd come out unscratched and flawless like they do in video games?"

"No," answered Matthew. Dad then turned his attention to him, pointing out that that was the most stupid thing he had ever done so far. He went on for a while before Dominic joined in.

"Yeah, it really was," Dominic said.

Dad turned on him with the same tension he had toward Matthew. By the look on Dominic's face, I could tell that that wasn't the reaction he was expecting from Dad. Scolding followed, Dad saying that he was no better for throwing his own brother under the bus. By that time, my throat was getting itchy, so itchy that I needed to cough. But I knew that if I did anything at all to catch his attention, it would be my turn to get lectured.

"But Dad, you taught me to be honest!" Dominic protested.

"There are times to be honest and there are times to keep quiet, Dominic! Which do you think this time is supposed to be?"

Dominic dropped his face, but Dad's glare was on him. I couldn't hold it in anymore. I coughed. And what I expected happened.

Dad turned to me. It was my turn to hear what I did

wrong. "Veo! You're the oldest! How could you let your brothers do something so stupid?!"

My mouth hung open. He seemed to think that I wasn't throwing rocks, but I was. Regardless, I still was at fault for allowing them to do this.

"What? Why is it my fault now?" I asked, not realizing what I was setting myself up for. Dad was scary when he got mad. But anyone knew the scariest and loudest came after a chuckle that was forced.

And there it was, that low chuckle, followed by, "Why is it your fault now?"

I should have stayed quiet.

I WAS LYING on the futon when I heard Dad's favorite song come on. An upbeat song that I could only assume he put on to calm his nerves.

Queen Marie stepped on me
A poor fish that man could never see
Crush the coral, feed the sea
Red water that bring big ones to my territory
Please, please, Queen Marie,
Please go back home

It was near midnight, and the lectures had stopped two hours ago. I blew my tongue out as I watched the shadows and lights underneath the door. I didn't deserve to get scolded. And although I didn't care much about going to

Saipan, especially since I'd be seeing Mom, Matthew and Dominic didn't deserve to lose that opportunity. But then again, she didn't care, so maybe it was a good thing that we lost the trip. I shut my eyes, remembering the night that she decided I wasn't worth having around.

Uncle Mike was her brother, someone I looked up to. He was always on adventures with the sea, experimenting with parachutes and jet skis. He was the one who led hikes in our family, traveling to and from every country in Asia. He even had two daughters and a son, who I knew he loved because he always got them something from every trip he made. An epic guy. *The epic guy.* The one who actually lived life to the fullest. I tried to do what he did. I tried to learn kung fu when he was learning it. I managed to break a piece of wood, but I also came in with a bloody hand that resulted in Mom yelling at me and Uncle Mike after she fixed my hand up. He also once brought me to the roof of Grandma's house to look at the starry night, but it ended with a caved in roof and, again, with a yelling mother as Grandma shook her head at Uncle Mike. My mom always had a low opinion of him. I suppose she didn't notice how much I admired him until she caught me sneaking into his room at night to ask for his bike. I thought she was sound asleep in hers.

"Uncle Mike, can I borrow your bike—" I sang once I set foot past his door. I cut my thought short when I saw Mom hovering over Uncle Mike with a furious spark in her eyes that shut me up in an instant. The room smelled weird, but Uncle Mike didn't even seem stunned at the situation. His posture and his face screamed defeat at Mom's angry mode ruining his night and mine. She pushed me out the room, scolded Uncle Mike, then scolded me outside an hour later for not being in bed.

"You never listen to me, boy. You're just making things harder than it is," she clicked her tongue, shaking her head at me. The next day, she told me I was going back to Guam. Even though she cried at the airport, I could tell my moving away would ease her off her parenting duties. What a great mom.

"Veo, are you awake?" whispered Matthew.

I didn't answer, keeping my eyes on the shadows that were underneath the door. They weren't moving, but I still watched them.

"Dominic?" Matthew whispered.

"Yeah?" he answered.

"I'm thinking that we could buy our own tickets," Matthew whispered. I stayed quiet as I listened to their conversation.

"With what money?" asked Dominic.

"Maybe we could work. Mow people's lawns. Barbecue for them. Or maybe we could ask them to donate for our trip."

"That will take too long."

It *would* take too long. And although I didn't think a trip to Saipan was worth the trouble, my brothers thought so. And Matthew was on to something. We could still go to Saipan. We just had to think of a different way of getting there. But how?

I kept listening as they whispered on and on. Dad's favorite song repeated itself so many times. But when I actually listened, the song planted a genius idea in my head.

I jumped up and out of the futon, and onto Dominic's bed. "You guys! I know how we can see Mom in Saipan!"

"How?" Matthew asked with his face upside down from the top bunk, looking at me.

"Yeah, how?"

"We're going to sail there!"

It was easy to get my brothers to agree that this was the best way to see Mom. It was the only way that, if we excelled at it, we could see her anytime of the year. "Oh, man! Mom will be so happy. We'll be like the old Chamorros!" Matthew laughed after we decided our adventure would start the next night.

THE NIGHT WIND hit me. It was colder than usual. Maybe it was all in my head because I knew that whenever I traveled, everything got colder. Or maybe it was the night being colder than other nights. I didn't realize that I was freezing until I glanced at my brothers who were doing the same thing.

"Maybe we should get our jackets," Dominic suggested with a light shiver.

"It'll soak up the ocean water if we fall in. And it will take up too much space if we take it off. It'll be useless."

Matthew agreed in a low voice. His posture gave off a hint of hesitancy already. But this was the beginning of every adventure: uncertainty. I had to perk them up, make them dream of the finish line.

"Come on, guys! We're going to see Mom!" I said with

a huge smile that rubbed off on Matthew. But Dominic kept looking back at the closed front door and screen door. As Matthew picked up our tools and materials, I asked, "Do you want to see Mom, Dominic?"

He nodded before I reassured him that this trip would be worth it. For the only time all night, he listened to me.

Buddy appeared from under our trailer house, wagging his tail. As we started our journey down the hill, he followed us. I thought he was doing a good job being our guard dog, but Matthew pointed out that we wouldn't have enough space for Buddy. Realizing he was right, I told Buddy to stay and watch over Dad. A successful command to our new guard dog.

We walked down the hill and I ran through the checklist of things we had and what we would need. We had it all though.

- ✓ Three coconuts
- ✓ Knife
- ✓ Machete
- ✓ Three bottles of water
- ✓ One bag of chips
- ✓ Rope

We stopped by the gas station to get a pallet made of plywood, then we were off to the beach that was right across the street.

The night was even chillier by the beach, but I tried not to show it. Dominic, though, had his hands wrapped around his arms, trying to keep warm. Once Matthew noticed, he did the same.

The beach was dark. There were no streetlights shining onto it. I swear I could have opened and closed my eyes, and I would have seen the exact same thing either way.

Close. Open. Close. Open. Darkness. Darkness. Darkness. Darkness.

We managed to find a spot with some lights. I pushed the pallet onto the water and put our plastic bags of items on it. We had enough room for us, and I figured it wouldn't be a long journey. The flights from Guam to Saipan were only 30-45 minutes long. A boat ride, I assumed, would take twice as long, so we'd be on Saipan by an hour.

"Come on, guys!" I said as I got on.

Dominic glanced back and forth. "I want to go back."

"No! Why?" I asked.

"I want to go back," he repeated shakily. There was fear in his voice, which soon took over his face. "I want to go back. I'll fly there instead."

"Hey, come on, Dominic. We have to do this for Mom." I got off the pallet but dropped into the water. My whole body was soaked, and now the cold air was even chillier. I couldn't hide my shivering this time.

My brothers noticed this right away, and as I came closer to them, they backed away. Dominic began crying. "I want to go home!"

I held on to Matthew's wrist. "Matthew, you still want to sail to Saipan, right?" But water dripped onto his wrist, and those tiny specks of water gave him a hint of how much colder he could get if he kept on. "Don't you?" I asked.

"I do," he said as he teared up. "But I want to go home too." And soon, he joined in crying with Dominic.

I grew frustrated, muttering all I could about what

kind of adventurers my brothers were. But it was all useless. I wouldn't venture out with anyone else, and there was no way I could get my brothers onto the pallet board now. Even if I did, they wouldn't be fearless enough to handle any problems that could come up, like sharks or pirates.

I sucked up my pride as I told them to follow me, heading back to the gas station. I asked to use their phone, and when Dad answered, he was already mad enough to yell on the line.

BY THE TIME we got home, Dad was still yelling. I stood in the living room with my brothers as I listened.

"You boys don't know how to sail! You could have died out there!"

"I know," I answered in a low tone.

"What did you think was going to happen, boy? What? Were you going to reach your dream spot in an hour? It's not an airplane."

I didn't answer. But he stood there, waiting. And although it rang true for my brothers and not for me, it came out of my mouth anyway. "We just wanted to see Mom."

From there, the bubbles from his boiling mind ceased. He sighed as he rubbed his face. It took a while, but when he opened his mouth to say something, all that came out was, "Go to bed."

I got to bed after I changed out of my wet clothes.

Then I fell asleep after watching the still shadows underneath the door again.

THE FOLLOWING DAY, Dad said nothing about our adventure. My brothers and I went outside to play with Buddy. Dad didn't hold us back from enjoying the day. We even went inside afterward and played with his guitar, the one thing he never wanted us to touch. He saw us trying to play a chord, but with our fingers being too short to do certain chords, he only grinned.

Eventually, Matthew and Dominic resigned themselves to the fortress they built out of boxes and pillows inside our bedroom. But I stayed longer, trying to learn the instrument that Dad played with ease. He had this ability to recreate any tune by simply hearing it. It was like he created the sheet music in his head without it ever being printed on paper. That trait of Dad's was something my mom even pointed out. "It's a skill not every musician has, boy," her voice sang in my head. I rolled my eyes at the imagined sound of her voice.

"You hungry, son? There's still some leftovers," Dad asked, holding the pot of *tinaktak* in the kitchen.

"I'm not. You can eat it, Dad."

I could only hear him sigh as I played the guitar, which made me stop altogether. "Are you okay, Dad?"

"I'm okay," he said, not convincing me in the slightest. I nodded, thinking that maybe we had let him down somehow. Thinking back to the day before, I thought that maybe he felt like we would choose Mom over him, but that wasn't true. I knew it wasn't. I'd stick with him over her any day.

"Dad?"

He looked back at me.

"We just really wanted to see Mom. I'm sorry."

Dad told me that all was forgiven, that everything was okay and forgotten. But as he turned, I heard him say something I knew he wanted to keep to himself. So I said nothing about it, returning to the guitar.

"I really wanted to see her too," he'd said quietly.

TRACK #4
Three on a Match

When I was 11 years old. . .

THIS SONG WASN'T ever played in the moments I connect it to. It was a song that played in my head when the moments were happening. It was like a love song attaching itself to a dance under the moon or a religious song to a worship moment in church. I think the lyrics had something to do with it, but I don't know exactly. It just did. Whenever I heard it play, these moments surface, ones that I always tried to push to the back of my mind.

We were two on a match on Sunday
Sat in our spots as always
But a third joined in before I lit
And now, we're three on a match on Sunday

By this time, I was in the fifth grade. Dad found a job months ago, and I thought he was enjoying it. He seemed like he was. But he couldn't make enough to pay the power bills every month, so the house was always without power for a few weeks until he could make the payment. But I didn't mind. Neither did Matthew or Dominic.

Matthew was in the bathroom, Dominic was at a speech competition practice for school, and I was sitting on the couch, trying to learn how to play Dad's guitar when a stranger came knocking on the screen door.

"Knock, knock," he said as he tapped on the metal part of the screen door. "Where's your dad?"

"Who are you?" I asked.

"I'm Joaquin, but you can call me Tito. Where's your dad?"

I yelled for Dad, which it didn't take much effort with the thin walls of our home. Whenever someone was pooping in the bathroom, everyone knew it. Everyone could hear each fart coming out of the pooper's butt.

Dad came out. "Hey, what the hell. . ." he whispered to the stranger. "You're not supposed to be here." Then he was past the screen door, shoving the visitor down the steps.

"Ouch! I know! Par! But I need some help," Tito said. Their conversation simmered down to whispers until Dad asked him, "Fine. Where is it?" then disappeared into the yard. I kept toying with the guitar until I heard a car engine starting and failing. I assumed Dad was helping Tito with a car problem.

I hurried outside to watch Dad's superhuman ability to lift a car. Believe it or not, he could do it. I got out there in time to see him lift the front end of the vehicle. As he continued lifting it, Tito got to his knees and peered under the poorly maintained sedan.

"I'm telling you, Tito. There's a problem with your battery," Dad said. But Tito wasn't listening. He was convinced that the problem was under the car. "Maybe it's the tires," he suggested.

At that point, Matthew was also by the screen door. "What are you doing?"

"Learning," I answered.

"Learning what?"

"How to fix a car."

Matthew pushed by me and ran out to them, saying, "Dad, I want to know how to fix a car!" But Dad didn't say anything right away. It took a few moments until he told us to go to Uncle Dun's house down the road to borrow his tools.

"But I want to learn how to fix a car!" Matthew whined.

Tito came out from underneath the car with his lips parted, looking at Matthew in a way that I found creepy. His teeth were black and incomplete inside his chapped, dry mouth. His hair was long and looked as if he never combed it and his eyes moved so fast that they'd make him a winner in a race if they had one for eyes. "Get the stuff and we'll teach you how to fix a car," he said.

Matthew's eyes darted back and forth to Dad and the creepy man. It was one of those moments where I knew he didn't know what to say or do. We'd just met this man. His look of confusion froze until I got up and said, "Come on, Matthew. Let's go."

We started down the road. He looked back at Dad every now and then to check on him until he was out of sight. "Who is that?" he finally asked me.

"I don't know," I answered, hoping the topic would drop right then and there.

Uncle Dun didn't live far, so the topic did drop as soon

as Matthew saw him on his lawn, scanning the walls of his home.

"Uncle Dun!" Matthew called out before running to him. I kept at my own pace, but when I got to them, Uncle Dun was already by his pick-up truck gathering his tools.

"Did you ask him already?" I asked. Matthew nodded with an energy that wasn't there a minute ago.

"Little Man," Uncle Dun greeted me. I bowed my head to amen him when he pinched my nose the way he usually did, bringing a smile to my face. I knew I'd do that to my nephews and nieces someday. "I'm working on fixing up my house, starting with a good paint job. Think you boys can handle it today?"

"Oh, cool! What color are you going to paint it?" Matthew asked. But his question went unnoticed as I matched his excitement, saying that I'd paint it faster than he would. Of course, Matthew took on the challenge too, but Uncle Dun told us to give the tools to Dad before our match began.

"I'll race you there!" Matthew said. We ran back to our house with the tools and then back to Uncle Dun's place. He was blasting music through a speaker in his garage, a beginning marker of our single-color paint day duel.

WE WERE FINISHING up the paint job by the time the sun was setting. Uncle Dun had gone inside to look for something while Matthew and I put the paint rollers and other tools away in his garage. The walls weren't the only things coated in paint. Our faces were too. By the time we finished putting things away, we were back to laughing at how messy we were. The winner of the challenge though? Undetermined. Everything looked one color. There was no way to tell who painted what part of the house. I didn't know how we would determine the winner, and I felt pretty stupid for thinking it was a painting contest. But it was a fun day regardless.

Uncle Dun came out, counting money in his hands. "17, 18, 19, 20. . . here, boys. Ten dollars for Matthew and ten dollars for Veo."

"Whoa! Thanks, Uncle Dun!" Matthew and I both said, surprised that we were getting money at all. As Matthew danced around, counting the many bills in his hands, my thoughts became vocal. "Why are you giving us money?"

"Because you boys helped out, and I know things are tight around your house for now. So use the money I gave you wisely."

"Thank you!" Matthew said, giving him a hug. He bounced up and down after, running around while I stood still, thinking of how often I had money in my hands. "Thank you, Uncle Dun. This means a lot."

He messed up my hair before telling me to go back home. We waved at him as we left. "Guess what, Veo," Matthew said on our walk back.

"What?"

"I'm going to be a painter when I grow up!"

I scoffed. We were still kids and painting a house was easy. It must be ten times easier for adults to finish the job!

I said that thought too. But Matthew's spirits were so high from being paid to paint that my reasoning couldn't bring him back down to Earth.

"It doesn't matter, my brother! I will find a way to get paid for my painting abilities! Laugh all you want now, but I'll be making more money than you soon!"

As he expected, I laughed. I never told him this, but I hoped that he'd be right, that someday he'd get paid for whatever he wanted to do, whether that was painting or not. I grinned as he kept on because it was nice to see a brother that dreams.

By the time we reached our place, Dad and Tito were still there. They were sitting in the garage. The tools were sitting on top of a table, and the car was silent. I couldn't tell if it was fixed or not, but the sun was half gone and would be completely gone in the next three minutes. Their attempt at the car was done for the day.

"Veo, Matthew," Dad started. "You're going to spend the night at Auntie Connie's tonight."

"What? Why?" Matthew asked. I glanced at Tito, who had a haunted look in his eyes and whose gaze avoided everyone else's.

"Because Keoni is there. He just flew in."

"Oh, no way!" Matthew exclaimed. "Today is such a great day!" I felt some excitement, but above that was curiosity about Tito.

Keoni was our cousin who we hadn't seen in years. He moved to the States to live with his aunt and uncle, and he only came every other year during summer. He was early this year, but I wasn't about to complain. Every time we got to play with Keoni, problems and games were funnier. He was that lively.

"Go, clean yourselves up, then head over. They're expecting you," Dad said, smiling.

"What about Dominic?" I asked.

"Sleeping over at Reggie's house."

I followed Matthew's trail inside, took a shower after he did, and grabbed whatever I thought we needed. After kissing Dad good night, we headed over with the sky dark with clouds overhead.

"Hi, Auntie Connie!" Matthew said when she opened the door, but she held up a finger to her lips, shushing us.

"Keoni is sleeping," she whispered as she let us in. "But he'll be up soon. Dinner is about ready."

"Can we see him?" Matthew asked. Auntie Connie pointed to his room after telling us to let him sleep until she finished cooking. We snuck into his dark room. Matthew turned a lamp on, which failed to wake him up. By the looks of the room, it was prepared for our appearance tonight with covered futon mats on the floor.

Matthew put his stuff on a chair nearby and lay down, counting his money over and over again. He might as well have laughed, saying "He-he-he. I got money," because I knew he was thinking it. I joined him on the other futon. But soon, Matthew lay on his side, telling me not to bother him. According to him, he wanted to nap before they woke up for dinner, which didn't make sense, but whatever. I figured that he'd stay asleep for the rest of the night. The day had been busy for us both.

As I counted my money that always amounted to $10, I wondered how I should use it. Uncle Dun said to spend it wisely, but I'd never had this much money before, so spending it wisely was something I didn't know how to do. Should I spend it on candy? On toys that I would have asked Dad for? But what made a "wise" decision with money? I got up and headed for the kitchen where Auntie Connie was stirring something in a large boiling pot.

"Auntie Connie?"

"Hmm?"

"How would you spend $10?"

She looked back before returning to her stirring. "Why do you ask?"

"Because I got $10 from Uncle Dun and he said to spend it wisely."

Auntie Connie took a wooden spoon off the counter and took a sip of her cooking before turning to me. "I wouldn't necessarily say to 'spend' it wisely, but to 'use' it wisely. You could use it to help your dad with things around the house."

My eyes lit up as I remembered our sailing adventure a while ago. Maybe I could make it up to him for that moment. "Thanks, Auntie Connie! I'll be back!"

I swiftly headed out the door before she could call me back from going out in the dark. She'd let it go if it meant she had to leave the stove. I was going to see Dad anyway, so there was no reason for her to follow me.

The lights weren't on in the garage since there was no power. I thought nothing of it. But once I made it from the steps to the locked front door, I found no candles lit in the living room. I peeked into the bathroom and my shared bedroom. No lights again. I circled the house to find one lit room. Dad's. I stood on top of the pick-up truck that was parked right by the window, curious to find out what was inside. Through one clear spot on the blurry window, I saw Tito and Dad sitting on opposite ends of the room. My eyes widened as I watched. Dad was cleaning a glass item. It was an item that I recognized in a class presentation from some adults in uniform who told us not to do a certain thing. Tito took out a small bag of something I thought I'd never see near Dad. A crystal-looking drug.

My mouth hung open as I watched, disbelieving that it was Dad in there. I knew what meth was. I knew what cocaine was. I knew what drugs were. And I knew their effects. I figured that maybe this was something that he did for certain occasions. Maybe he only did this for fun a few times a year. That wouldn't be so bad. Would it?

I tried to reassure myself that Dad knew what he was doing.

But he put money down on the table before taking a few bits of the drug and placing it in the pipe. Tito took the money, putting it in his pocket as I felt my blood boiling as I watched. He was stealing from us. This creepy man was stealing from us. But Dad. Dad was the one giving the creepy man our money.

I gripped my money in my hand, realizing where the money he was making went before he even paid the power bill. If he wouldn't pay the power, how long would it take for him not to pay for groceries? Then, Matthew and Dominic came to mind. I imagined them living in a home that had no power because of an adult who chose drugs over electricity. I knew Matthew looked up to him. How would this change things? How would this influence him? Would this limit Dominic with whatever he wanted to do?

So many questions scattered in my mind, raising my heat and anger.

I looked away to the road with a numb sensation spreading through my body. All I felt was rage as I fought back tears. But I waited, fighting my paralyzed limbs, knowing what I had to do.

Once Dad and the creepy man were knocked out in the living room, I broke in through his bedroom window. I scoured for every last drug in the house, including what was in the creepy man's bag. Then I climbed back out the window, dragged our metal trash bin across the street into the darkness, and lit the bag on fire. The air smelled weird, but familiar. I tried not to breathe too close to it. But I still stood straight, staring at the things that were keeping my family from making ends meet.

If he couldn't find it, he wouldn't do it. Dad was smarter than this.

ABOUT TWO MONTHS later, I came home from school alone. Dominic was still on with the speech competition and Matthew was taking extra classes after school. There was a possibility that he would get held back, but I wasn't sure. Dad kept me away from those things. He'd kept me away from quite a few things ever since that night. When he was searching the house for the stuff the following day, he saw me staring at him.

"Veo, have you seen a bag here?" he asked.

My eyes dropped. I couldn't believe he was asking me.

I looked back up at him and said, "Yes." He stared back. I could tell that he wanted to ask where it was, but he didn't.

As I kept walking home, I found myself feeling lonely walking without either of my brothers. But they were doing things that would help them, so it was worth a few walks alone. I reached our place and the air held that familiar scent that I'd smelled months ago. I ran to the open window of Dad's bedroom, and I saw it. The pipe, the bag, and Dad lying on the bed next to the table.

My mind blanked out, as a swirl of thoughts and emotions surfaced all at once. In a second, I found myself in the house, in Dad's bedroom, punching his face. I yelled. I screamed. "What are you doing? Dad, what are you doing? What's the matter with you?! You're going to mess us up like this!"

Dad stood up and shoved his hand against my face. I fell back onto the wall, crying, but I ran back at him. My eyes were on his big, dead eyes that kept moving just like the creepy man's. For a moment, I felt like he was lost, like his spirit had shrunk and lost itself in a vacuum of darkness inside his physical body that was filled with crystals. An astronaut detached from his spaceship, floating among the stars that made him wonder at beauty but feel no purpose. I could say anything, and it would feel like Dad wouldn't hear it as he swam in that confusion of space. I could tell that to him, but I could also tell that I wasn't worth fighting the crystals anymore.

But my tears built up as I opened my mouth anyway. "I don't care if you don't care about me anymore. But damn it! Care about Matthew and Dominic!"

Dad turned around and walked out. I called after

him, but he didn't look back. I ran outside once I heard the engine of his pick-up start. It roared louder than usual, louder than I could ever yell as it disappeared down the road.

TRACK #5
July Nights

When I was 21 years old. . .

I GLANCED AT the clock on the side table—10:15 a.m. It was no use. I told myself not to look at the time again and to just enjoy my day off from both my jobs. Yes, I worked two jobs within months of returning home. I needed to help with the medical bills, an unfortunate addition to a life back on this island with a sick dad who was more upbeat than ever. But the good news was that Hannah wasn't here, a fact that always made a cheer go off in my head.

The corners of my lips curved. I took note of my breathing as I studied the room. Our old bedroom was stripped of the bunk bed. Two twin-sized beds replaced it, in need of washed sheets that sat in the corner of the room, taking up even more space. The same thin maroon curtains with tears from my childhood still covered the windows. And that smell of wood still filled the room as it did every other room.

I shut my eyes, remembering what it was like waking up in Seattle. The room would be messy, just the way I liked it. It'd be lit with however much light the sun decided to give the city for the day. But the blinds did a good job balancing the light in the room if the sun decided to make the city warmer than usual. The little portable heater would be on, releasing hot air if it was a cold day. And the sound from outside? It would either be silent with the occasional ambulance sirens or humming with birds singing in the tall trees nearby. It was all beautiful (if it wasn't winter). But once I turned my head to see the face of a beautiful girl with her arms and legs reaching for all corners of the bed, leaving me with only enough room for half of my body on the bed, my mind would silence as my chest somehow reminded me of how I would feel at the end of the day: miserable. And the rain only made it worse, even though I'd thought that I'd be in love with water falling from the sky all my life.

I lay on my back, studying the wooden ceiling of my childhood bedroom. As I took a deep breath, I felt my pulse dance off my wrists. My eyes caught on its movement. The skin pushed up with each pulse. This should be a minor thing to take pleasure in watching. But with the beat and rhythm of the music that was growing louder and louder from the living room, I found my pulse dancing to the song.

Sugar, our nights in July
Oh, Baby, oh,
Why, oh, why
Let's go to that July night
Where I gave you your first kiss
Oh, Sugar, Sugarpie

The sound of footsteps hit the hollow floor outside the room. Soon, a sizzle came from beyond the bedroom door, accompanied by smoke entering the room from the gap underneath it. The room started to stink of bacon, cueing the start of my day.

When I came out, my dad said, "Finally, you're up," as he stood in front of the gas stove with tongs, looking perfectly healthy. I often wondered if he was really sick, but my payments for these hospital visits told me he was.

"Oy! Veo! You've been sleeping too long!" Matthew sang as he let the screen door slam behind him.

"Yeah, well, you know how it is to work."

"I know how to work one job. Not two. You look exhausted."

"I'm actually well-rested," I yawned. He rolled his eyes before taking the tongs from Dad, who went outside. I sat down in one of the chairs by the small dining table that stood behind the couch, rubbing my face and groaning. Working all day did sound exhausting, but the sleep after was always amazing. I reached for the corners of the room, feeling my body relax once I stopped.

"You don't have to do that, you know," Matthew said, unfazed as he turned the bacon over, the oil popping at him.

"Do what?"

"Work two jobs."

"Yeah, well, the bills say otherwise."

"Veo!" Dad called out from the garage.

I got up, heading for the screen door with another yawn, shutting my eyes. "Yeah, Dad?" And then, I heard her. It was easy to ignore messages, calls, and emails from her, but this—her laugh—was difficult to avoid. It sounded normal to everyone else, but having heard it so often, it tainted my appreciation of it, especially at the odd things it was directed at.

"You have such a gorgeous nose. It's no wonder where Veo gets it from," she said. My dad laughed and shook his head before turning his attention to me, hiding in the darkness of the screen door.

"Veo! You must remember your girlfriend, right? Hannah, is it?"

She laughed again, the kind of laugh that, again, would have sounded lovely to anyone else but me.

FALLING ON MY bed pushed the air out of me, but I needed it. The lights were shut off. I couldn't thank the dark curtains any more for completely covering the windows to hide me from all that was happening. I could safely say that my day off was going to waste as I heard my dad and brothers telling Hannah stories outside. There isn't a rule about ex-girlfriends and families hanging out. But it certainly feels weird that there isn't one in place.

The door opened. But with my arm the only form of comfort for my eyes, I didn't bother to look up.

"Hannah's nice," Dominic said. He had a curious grin that I knew was targeted at my situation. It was one that I should have known was coming, since she was a crazy bitch.

I didn't say anything. I'd had this conversation with

people before who actually got to know her. They'd always back her when she opened up about me being a lousy boyfriend, and maybe I was. But that wasn't an excuse for her to be a lunatic girlfriend.

"She's hot too," he laughed, leaving me to groan. It was a theory of mine that it was the pretty people who had it easy, who had people automatically on their side. It was proving correct with Hannah and everyone I encountered.

There was bustling in the closet as I finally looked up. "What are you doing?" I asked.

"Your girlfriend wants to—"

"Not my girlfriend."

"She's not your girlfriend?" He raised a brow at me, but I wasn't going to answer. "Oh, my brother! Your girlfriend. Your ex. Either way, she wants to cook for Dad tonight."

Mumbling curses in disbelief, I stood up to peek out the window. "What the hell."

"You know, you never mentioned anything about her since you came back, right?"

"Yeah, yeah. I know. It's biting me in the ass." I turned back to see Dominic pulling his wallet out of his bag. Before giving me a piece of advice and leaving the room, he chuckled as he held himself with the confidence that he'd grown over the years. "You might as well tell Dad what happened with her. It looks like he's falling in love with her, or the idea of her as his daughter."

I sighed, turning back to the window in the empty room. At that point, I'd be surprised if he asked her to leave, especially after what I did the last time I saw her. But I watched as Hannah got up from the white chair, saying something that I couldn't make out. Dominic passed, and soon they left in Matthew's car.

I kept mumbling curses as I headed to the front screen door. "Dad," I called out. "Is she gone?"

"She's coming back."

"But is she gone?"

He tipped the chair back to check. "Yeah, they left." His eyes locked on me as I opened the screen door and sat on the steps. There was a grin on his face, waiting for a story, one that had been waiting for months to be revealed. My dad followed some, if not most, conventions of masculinity. But there were several times in Saipan where I came out at midnight to get a glass of water only to see him watching soap operas. He was one for drama, and I knew he would never admit it.

"Hey, wait! Hold on!" Matthew yelled from the bathroom. I knew he wanted to hear the story too, but I started without him. Anyone could hear from the bathroom window anyway. Just had to listen hard enough.

IT WAS ABOUT two weeks after Matthew called me with the news of our dad. I knew where I was moving to in a month, and Hannah seemed to think so too, but she really didn't. The plan she came up with was for her to move to California that Friday morning. She would stay with her friends and search for a place to move into before I came over, which would be two weeks later. I knew that I should have said something official since this move would result in a break-up, but I didn't. Maybe I was scared. Or maybe I knew that Hannah was someone I couldn't escape from. I didn't know.

The week before Hannah left, there was a knock on the door when she was at work. It was Ricky, the nineteen-year-old neighbor, asking for a lighter. After lending him one, he asked me to follow him to his place, which usually meant a couple of drinks. And since it was a Friday, why the hell not?

We sat on the balcony, overlooking the "sinking of the sun" as Ricky liked to put it. It felt nice. For a moment, I forgot about Hannah, the move, and the reason why I had to move. But for the split second that it resurfaced, it showed on my face. Ricky caught on, blinking slowly. "I'm sensing your troubled aura. What's the problem?"

"Nothing. Nothing at all." I knew then as I know now that I am a terrible liar. But it didn't matter. Ricky was just a neighbor who I drank with from time to time. He didn't need to know everything about me.

He nodded as he caught on. "Alright. You don't need to tell me. But you look like you need a good night."

"Yeah. I'd love a great night," I answered as I picked off at the bottle.

"Then let's go."

I shook my head, labeling the idea of a good night as something unobtainable in this city. "I'm good, man." But as I said that, I realized that I hadn't experienced Seattle. I hadn't experienced any other states either. And now, I wasn't going to have that easy opportunity because I'd be back on an island, miles away.

Ricky laughed, breaking my thoughts up and eventually getting me to crack a smile.

"Shit, man," I started. "I need a good night." So we planned a trip. Las Vegas. Menacingly, I set it for the day of Hannah's departure. I decided I'd tell her afterward and deal with her wrath then, if I ever talked to her again.

HANNAH'S LAST WEEK in Seattle was actually the most pleasant week we had. It was the calm before the storm. Even though I was anticipating the unpleasant messages and calls that were going to blow up my phone in a few weeks, excitement still filled me for the weekend trip.

The day finally arrived for Hannah's departure. But as we got ready for me to drop her at the airport, she got a call. She left the room shortly only to come back and tell me that her trip was postponed. They'd be rescheduling her on the next flight out that had an available seat. I knew that I should have canceled my trip, but I didn't. Stupid me. I tried to go through plans I had for the day without telling her about it. But I knew she noticed me packing clothes and when I was leaving the apartment, it was difficult not to answer her when she asked, "Where are you going?"

"Las Vegas," I admitted as I stepped out the door. But man, I should have stayed inside. Her accusations of me cheating on her skyrocketed to where all the neighbors could hear how terrible of a guy I was.

But I left anyway.

THE NEXT DAY, Hannah sat by me on the floor of my hotel room once I woke up with a buzzing head. The floor reeked of vomit that I wasn't sure was mine. Ricky and a couple of other people in the room I didn't recognize were there, unconscious. But I was clean. I even had clothes on that weren't mine. They looked and smelled new.

Hannah had a smile on her face as she caressed my arm, telling me to lay back on the pillow that I didn't even notice was there. I groaned as I lay back down.

"I flew over to make sure you didn't do anything you regretted," she said. Her voice was already ingrained in my mind as a nuisance. I rolled my eyes, knowing that I could take care of myself, and that she would use last night against me someday. "Oh yeah? Did I gamble all my money away?" I said, shaking her hands off my body.

She furrowed her brows before she stood and turned to walk toward the dining table. "I did my job well."

"'Well,' my ass," I mouthed as I sat up. I scratched my head, trying to rid myself of the headache, but it wasn't going away. I stood up, reaching for a cup in the cupboard. Turning the faucet on, I filled the cup with water when I saw a band on my ring finger. Panic started to rise as I tried to remember the night's events, but my head was stirring like thick mud. Nothing made sense. Nothing served as actual memories. I couldn't remember last night.

I turned around and my eyes must have popped out of my head once I saw Hannah admiring the band on her ring finger. "Hannah. . . what happened last night?"

She giggled, "We got married!"

My jaw dropped as she turned around. Sensing my distress, the look on her face shifted as she tried to console me. "Don't worry though, babe. I'll make sure to make you happy like you've always been, if not happier."

"Happy? You think I'm happy, Hannah?"

"Hey, hey, hey. Calm down. You were the one who insisted that we—"

"That we what? That we get married? Hannah, I don't even like being with you. We always fight when I open my mouth to tell you about my day. And that's all because you get jealous because I worked with a girl. We argue when I tell you that I'm not hungry and you are, because you don't want to eat alone even though I'm still sitting at the table with you. And you get mad at me when I tell you I want to walk to the store by myself. And why is that? Because you think I'm going to another girl's house to do her. Hannah, we're terrible together!"

Her nostrils flared as she took a breather. It didn't happen often, but when it did, I knew she was choosing her words carefully. And I knew I ought to be grateful, but I wasn't. I wasn't thinking. "So what, Veo? We're moving to California together and we're already married. What's the point in getting a divorce?"

Out came the truth. "I'm not moving to California anymore. I have to move back home because my dad's sick. And Hannah, I don't want to be with you anymore. I just fucking can't," I said before I walked out the door.

Dad chuckled, leaning his elbow on the arm of the chair. Matthew threw his head back laughing. "So she's my sister-in-law?"

I was about to say no when I remembered that I never actually got a response from her about an annulment. I cursed under my breath, thinking that of all the times to push her out of my head, the useful times I shouldn't have, I did. "I asked for an annulment, but she never gave me an answer."

"Well, maybe she's going to give you an answer now," Dad said. "Is that why you never mentioned her?"

"Kind of. The main reason was because she sends demons to me even when I'm just thinking of her."

His brow knitted as Matthew laughed. Dad already liked her. And I was sure that the one night off that I had to myself was going to be spent with my ex-girlfriend who was also my wife. "Matthew," Dad called, stopping Matthew from laughing, "Go chop up some wood."

I could tell that Matthew sensed the seriousness in Dad's voice, so he left after grabbing the machete. It was me and Dad, alone now. It got silent. His eyes told me he was still full of thoughts, making the air uncomfortable. Not wanting to sit in it, I went inside.

I knew I was a terrible person for doing that to Hannah, for leaving for Las Vegas the day she left for California. I was a horrible boyfriend and now, a horrible husband. But as I plopped down on the couch, trying to rub the stress off my face, I recalled the message she sent me before I asked for the annulment.

I'm sorry. I don't need to be married to you to prove that I love you. Take all the time you need. . . for us and for your dad. I'll always be here for you. I love you.

I took a deep breath, trying to tell myself that this was the right thing to do. I wasn't happy, so I needed to break things off. But seeing someone so desperate for my company and love would always make me feel like I needed to stay, even when I knew I was toxic for her and she was for me.

Crap.

I thought of how I could break things off tonight, but with all the strength I had, I didn't even want to think about how to do it. I didn't want to ruin anyone's night. I headed for the bedroom to pack my things and ask any one of my friends if I could sleep over for the night.

Nobody replied right away, but that wasn't going to stop me. I would take Matthew's car and sleep on the beach if I had to.

The front screen door slammed shut accompanied by the sound of Hannah's laughter. She was talking to Dominic about something. I couldn't make it out, and honestly, I didn't want to know, so I continued packing.

"Hannah?" I heard Dad's voice.

"Yes?" she answered in a sweet tone. "You know, you seem very healthy for someone who's supposed to be sick."

That was a weird thing to say to anyone who was sick, but Dad didn't let it get to him. "Thanks," he said.

I heard mumbling, then the screen door shutting again. I figured that Dominic left the house before Dad continued. "*Nen*, I don't think it's a good idea for you to be here."

"What? Why? It's not because of Veo, is it?"

I couldn't hear an answer from Dad, so I pressed my ear against the door, trying to listen harder.

"Look, Hannah, if you want to fix things with my son, please fix them on your own time with him."

"I see," Hannah said. I heard plastic bags and glass bottles clinking. Then footsteps. Then the front screen door slammed again.

She'd gotten kicked out of her ex's house by her ex's dad.

I emerged from my bedroom, looking at my dad. I was surprised and grateful to him at that moment, but I forced myself to run, calling after Hannah.

The reason why things were so fuzzy between us was because I hadn't made things clear for her. And that's how all relationships should end: clear and blunt. There was no way to let someone down easy, so I must do it in the most brutal way possible.

Be an asshole.

She was by her rental car by the time she heard me calling her name. Her hope must have grown once she saw me running because her face lit up. She waited for whatever I had to say, though I knew she wasn't going to like it. But I had to rip the bandage off. Hopefully, this time, to the point where even lawyers couldn't find a loophole.

"Hannah, I want an annulment or divorce, whichever. And I'm breaking up with you. I don't want to be in a relationship with you. I'm finished with this, with me and you."

She was stunned. Another stunt by the asshole boyfriend/husband/ex-boyfriend/yet-to-be-ex-husband of hers. She was growing angry, and about to open her mouth to say something. But she must have seen something behind me to stop or maybe she finally realized what we had was not worth salvaging.

"We'll talk later then," she said before getting in her rental car and driving off.

"WHAT A DAY off, huh?" Matthew said as he flipped the chicken on the barbecue grill.

I smiled. "Yeah. What a day off." Tomorrow, I had to return to two different jobs, two shifts in one day. I sighed, bracing myself for it.

"You should quit those jobs you're working," Matthew said.

"Because we're so rich, right?"

He chuckled before heading inside. I thought that was the end of the conversation as I followed him in. But once I shut the screen door behind me, he handed me a folded piece of paper. It was one of his check stubs with an amount that was more than I was getting at both of my jobs put together.

"Holy. . ." I couldn't tell if both of my jobs were paying their employees low amounts or if this job Matthew was working was just too good. But it didn't matter. He was getting paid higher as a dishwasher than I was as a cook.

"They have an opening."

"Whatever it is, I'm up for it. Front of house. Back of house. Dishwasher. Whatever. I'll do it."

"Yeah? Awesome. The application is online. It's called Kikki's Breakfast House."

It was a typical name for a restaurant. Nothing impressive. But the name of a workplace was never a selling or breaking point for me, so I told him that I'd apply that same night. "Ey! Two of the Mafnas brothers take on Kikki's!" Matthew cheered. I laughed, eventually cheering with him.

"Don't let the managers introduce you to everyone. I'll do that on your first day, Brother. I'll show you all the easy chicks, the *nampas*, the cool ones, and everyone else!"

"Whatever you say," I laughed before hearing Dad yell from outside.

"Oy! Veo! Come out here and barbecue this since your wife isn't here!" he said, bringing a grin to my face. It was an actually funny thing to hear from him on my day off.

I went outside, gratefully taking the tongs from him. But as the night went on, my memories of him made an appearance again, bringing my guard up. Even though he showed me he changed, my wall was something that would take a lot to tear down.

TRACK #6
Everybody's Talkin'

When I was 12 years old...

VAL WAS STANDING by the back of the mall after school. She was out of her uniform, dressed in shorts and a tank top with shoes and long socks that elongated her legs. She looked different, the kind of different that I shouldn't be thinking of since she was my cousin. But I noticed her.

On a regular day, I would have taken the school bus home, but I decided to go to the mall instead. I didn't want to be home, since both my brothers had something to do after school. If I went home, I'd be either alone or with Dad. And even if he decided to be funny and pleasant today, I didn't want to be around him. The only time I'd want to be around him is if Dominic and Matthew were there, so he couldn't mess them up. Harsh, I know. Maybe it was a teenager thing. Or maybe the little visit from the cops for a presentation that day in school set me off.

"So we were supposed to have this presentation last week, but they canceled since things came up. But every class must see this presentation, so they popped in today with no warning," Mr. Manglona growled in class. "So today, we are visited by Officer Frank and Officer Lahey and their dog. But before they come in, I have to warn you: you cannot touch the dog. I repeat, *you cannot touch the dog*. Okay? Are we clear?"

There was only a murmur of answers from the class.

"I said, 'Are we clear on that?'"

"Yes, sir," we all answered.

He nodded and the police officers came in.

The cops did the usual speech that I would expect from any presentation. The dos. The don'ts. The how-to-deal with situations. The boring things in these presentations. But they mentioned that drugs were a big deal, and that if anybody in our families or among our friends was doing them, or if we were doing them, we were in harm's way.

I thought I'd only scoffed in my mind, but people started looking at me, including Officer Frank.

"Excuse me?" he said.

My brow lifted. "Yes?"

"Do you have a problem with what we do here?"

"No?" I said slowly. "Not at all."

"Then keep your reactions to yourself, boy."

By that time, everybody was looking at me. I only nodded. There was no need to stir up anything else. But I heard snickering.

Eventually, they brought in the dog that sniffed through all our things and all of us. I continued watching him as the cops finished their presentation. He was a smart dog.

"If you see any suspicious behavior, call us." They handed out pieces of paper folded three ways that had all the things they had just told us. Finally, they left.

I suppose it served as a reminder for something that must be forgotten.

"Veo?" Val snapped me back into the present.

I turned to her, acting surprised. "Val?"

She laughed. "You know, you're such a bad liar. I know you saw me."

I scratched the back of my head with an embarrassed laugh. "Sorry. I haven't seen you in a while."

"It's been a couple of years. But you look good. You're growing up nicely, and I hear that crack in your voice."

My voice was one of the insecurities that held me back from talking to girls. It kept me in a state of wondering if my voice would forever crack. It was embarrassing even reading in class once a question in the text popped up. *Will WiLL ever feel that same lOve anD meet young TeREsa agAIn? (clears throat).*

"Right. Yeah. Well, I best be goi—"

"Wanna grab something to eat?"

"Uh, yeah, sure." I followed her in, sensing myself being awkward. I noticed a new height difference that wasn't there the last time I saw her. She was older, but I was taller.

"How's my dad?" she asked.

"Uncle Dun? He's alright. Working a lot, but he still comes over and drinks with my dad."

"Uh-huh. I see." She went on, asking about my brothers and the dreams she remembered us telling her about. She laughed when I told her that Matthew wanted to become a professional painter before we separated to get our food.

We came back to sit in a booth, talking about our younger days. We laughed at how slow Dominic was, how loud Auntie Connie got, and all that stuff. The smile on her face was genuine and it made me wonder. "Why'd you stop coming over?" I asked.

"Well, you see, Veo, when parents split, that usually means that their children are left with one or the other—"

"I got that, Val. But even though my dad split up with my mom, they made an effort for us to see my mom. Why don't you? Or do you? Maybe I never catch you."

At that point, Val sighed. Scratching the back of her head, she shrugged. It was obvious that she was uncomfortable. It took a few moments before she looked at me. Maybe I wrongly interpreted the look in her eyes, but it was a sexy gaze, despite the topic.

"My dad drinks, Veo."

"Yeah, I kinda got that. He drinks with my—"

"No, Veo. He *drinks*. A lot. It got to a point where he hit my mom after he threw our telephone on the floor so hard that it smashed into pieces. My mom got scared. I got fed up. But the thing is that my dad was like that for a long time. I just thought it was normal, seeing my mom get hurt."

Her eyes dropped to the floor as she fidgeted with her bracelets. Then she broke out of the stare and munched on a french fry with a grin.

"People never break out of bad habits, Veo. They just don't."

Her gaze on me made me feel uncomfortable but wanted—in a way that cousins shouldn't want each other. I continued with the conversation as best I could, before pushing myself to take the next bus home.

LIGHTS. VISION. IT's an odd thing. After being in a room for so long, my eyes craved another set of lights. In this case, I had been in the living room for two hours. The light bulbs were new today. But they were low-light and yellow. Not every corner of the room was lit even if all the lights were flicked on. Rats and cockroaches could hide under the dining table and nobody would notice. It wasn't a problem at first, but having to be yelled at in that badly lit room for so long caused my headache. Not the yelling. The light.

I don't actually remember what my dad was yelling at me that night about. Maybe it was for coming home late after a meal with my cousin and he didn't know my whereabouts. But I do remember seeing Matthew and Dominic still in their uniform. They were laughing and pointing at me from behind Dad.

"Yadda yadda, Veo! Listen, boy! Yadda yadda!" he scolded.

Dominic tended to snort the same way that I imagined a pig laughed. Silent laughter must have been difficult for him to keep, so he slipped a snort as he laughed behind my dad. Their faces adjusted in a split second when Dad turned around. His face was all scrunched up, directing his annoyance at them. Saying nothing, they both walked back to our bedroom, leaving me, Dad, and Buddy in the living room.

There was a long moment of silence between us once the bedroom door shut. I remember hearing Buddy panting on the sofa. His fur matched everything in the yellow room. I would have heard the crickets singing that night, and the bugs hitting against the metal trash bin outside. But Dad's music was playing in the corner of the room catching my attention.

Everybody's talkin'
All words drilling
Snapping, breaking
Can't hear what's being said

You've numbed my thoughts
Numbed my thinking
Drowning, drowning
Please don't leave me

I sat on the coffee table as I continued to watch my dad. At this point, I knew he must have been wondering whether to continue the yelling or not.

He chose to continue, a decision that annoyed me, as it came from the man who chose to feel good over the well-being of his sons. I couldn't tell if he was still using the stuff. He could be hiding it from me and smoking or snorting while we were all at school. What a grown-up thing to do.

I felt the stress on my forehead as I listened to him.

"Keep acting like a little kid, Veo, and I'll keep treating you like one," he said. It finally ignited me. I didn't have to listen to a druggie rant as I heard Val's voice in my head again. *People never break out of bad habits, Veo. They just don't.*

I stood up and headed for the bedroom.

"And where do you think you're going, Veo?" Dad said.

I looked back at him, glaring into his eyes that were closer to mine since I'd hit puberty. I felt anger in every bone and muscle in my body as I answered.

"I'm going to look for my pipe, or was it my needle? Whichever." My eyes locked onto his, challenging him to say whatever came to his failed father mind. But he averted his angry gaze to the floor.

I turned and closed the door behind me. He didn't follow me in. My brothers' attentions were locked on their drawings and homework. They didn't hear what I had said to Dad.

TRACK #7
Little Danny Grow

When I was 13 years old. . .

Someone asked Dad why his boys never got up at the end of Mass for the communion about a month ago. It was a question nobody really asked, so it caught him off guard as he realized that he never had us attend CCD. So that was where the brothers and I were on this beautiful Saturday morning. Inside a church. Being shushed whenever a sound came out of our mouths by Sister Lea. And it was the first of many Saturdays that was to come.

I didn't think much of church. I thought it was one of those things I had to do because everyone else did it. So I sat there, barely listening to Sister Lea talking about having faith in the Lord. My mind often scattered, diving into thoughts about whatever I was looking at. I don't remember most of what I thought about, but I do remember glancing over at one of my classmates from school. His name was Jesse. In the beginning of the school year, he was upbeat and open about his love for Jesus. The kind of person that I expected to go to those Protestant churches. But now, he was here, sitting in the row in front of me. He had eyes that, even if they filled with energy, wouldn't try to look at the priest or nun or anyone else around him. I could only theorize that this religion wasn't something he was into, so that only brought up another question: why was he here now?

"Shh!" Sister Lea broke my train of thought, as she glared at Matthew, who was apologizing after a laugh cut short by her scowl.

At recess, the whole class of kids went out to the tent-covered tables that were set up for us to eat our lunch. I left my brothers and walked over to Jesse who sat alone. He slouched with his chin, resting on his forearms on the table.

"Hi," I greeted him. But he didn't budge. He probably didn't hear me. "Hi there," I said again.

I saw his eyes move my way, but his head didn't turn.

"I'm Veo." I knew he must have known my name, but I said it anyway to break the ice, even for a little bit.

"Jesse."

"Mind if I sit?"

Jesse gestured at the open seat. It was an awkward starting point since we sat in silence for a bit. I didn't know what he liked. I never talked to him before, but he was my age, so he couldn't be too different from me. "So do you play any video games?" I asked.

He started out slow. It took more questions to get him to talk, but I got him there.

"My dad and my sister got me into it," he admitted before opening up to the point where I saw some spark of excitement.

He told me that his sister was more skilled with video games than he was, and that was what pushed him into playing more. He wanted to beat her score or beat her to the next level of whatever game it was for the month or so. But he also told me that whenever he and his sister couldn't solve a part of a game, that's where their dad came in. They would beg him to play it, then tell them how to win.

Somehow the topic switched over to sports and outdoor games. He was in Little League and his whole family would help him with his batting techniques. His dad would pitch baseballs. His mom, uncle, and sister would fetch the balls. It was something my dad wanted to do for Matthew but didn't because Dominic and I complained about it. It sounded like I'd missed out. I didn't dwell so much on it though, because the topic switched to birthdays. I didn't tell Jesse about my birthday that year, because I didn't remember how I spent it. But he told me that he had spent his in the hospital.

Jesse's face transformed back to how it was in the beginning of our conversation. His eyelids drooped as he rested his chin back on his forearms, closing me off.

"Why'd you spend it in the hospital?" I stupidly asked.

"My dad had a heart attack. He's in a coma right now."

Struck like a deer in headlights, I froze. I didn't know what to say. All I was thinking was that I probably shouldn't have opened that door for him. He chuckled as a tear rolled down his cheek. "I'm here because this is his church. He said that God wouldn't give me anything I couldn't handle. And he always told me that praying helps. I'm hoping it does."

The bell sounded behind me. It was time to return to

the lesson, and as bad as it sounds, I felt relieved that I didn't have to say any more on that topic. Even worse, I felt grateful that I wasn't him. It was a terrible thing to feel when I was supposed to be listening to him spill out the horrible things he was going through. But I couldn't help but reflect on my relationship with my dad.

Jesse wiped his nose on his sleeve before taking deep breaths and standing up. "Yeah. Well, it's time to go."

THE FOLLOWING SATURDAY, I stood outside the church, waiting for the heavy rain to die down. Jesse wasn't there that day and he wasn't in school the day before either. I didn't hear anything about his reason for being absent since nobody talked about him. But I could only assume that there was a change in his dad's condition. Maybe he got better and his whole family was celebrating, but something was telling me that he'd gotten worse. Much worse.

Class was still going on when I saw Val walking by with her head down. Each strand of hair and every piece of clothing was soaked in rainwater. But the smile in her eyes said she didn't mind, since she was walking slow. I pretended not to notice her again, but she spotted me once I'd averted my eyes.

"Hey! What are you doing here?" she asked, coming over.

I stood by, trying not to get wet. "CCD," I pointed inside.

"Why are you outside then? It looks like they're still

doing stuff. Are you skipping CCD class, Veo? Naughty, naughty," she teased, successfully pulling a laugh out of me.

"I guess so," I started. But before I went on, my mind rewound to the conversation I had with Sister Lea moments earlier. My thought on Jesse and his dad and the afterlife sparked something.

Me: "Miss Lea—"

Sister Lea: "Sister Lea."

Me: "Sorry. Sister Lea. If God is real, then why can't we see Him?"

Sister Lea: "Good question, Veo. Everyone, listen. God is real, and He is one of those Beings that we must have faith in believing is there. He's like the wind. You can't see the wind, can you, Veo?"

Me: "You can kind of see the wind. I know I can feel it. It even hits against things that make me aware—"

Sister Lea: "Then how about gravity? Can you see gravity?"

Me: "No. But there's science to prove gravity's existence."

Sister Lea: "Well, there you go. You don't need to see something to believe it's real. If you study hard enough, you'll also find scientific evidence for God. But you can always just have faith that He's there."

Me: "Do you have any scientific evidence for Him?"

Sister Lea: "I don't, Veo. I'm sorry. I'm not a scientist."

Me: "Then, Miss, uh, I mean, Sister Lea, God is good, right?"

Sister Lea: "All the time."

Me: "Then why does He let bad things happen?"

Sister Lea: "Bad things are tests for us all. To rely on Him when times are tough requires trust and faith. We must know that we can always make it past the bad times with Him by our side. Because there will always be a good day coming even if you can't see it."

Sister Lea had this smile on her face that said that she was pleased with her message. But I wasn't feeling the same way. By her definition of God, He was this all-powerful Being that needed to know He can trust us to trust Him. He was like those girlfriends on TV shows who tested their boyfriends who they suspected were cheating on them.

"So you going to go back in, or what?" Val asked, breaking me out of my thoughts.

"No. It's not really my thing."

"God's not your thing?" she laughed. "Can't say I blame you. I thought the same thing, but I still went on with CCD. I had nothing else better to do. You're a little old for it anyway."

I shrugged, still waiting for the rain to die down, but there was no sign that it would anytime soon.

"So what is it, dear cousin? What makes God not your thing?"

"He doesn't make sense. The idea of it all doesn't make sense. A god who is good in every way lets evil happen. How is that good?"

"Maybe since evil is already here, you need to go through the evil to get to the ultimate good."

"Why would I 'need' to go through it though? If God could do anything, He could rid all evil from the world. Couldn't He? Wipe it all clean for us all, so we could be together in the garden again. It just doesn't make sense. I'm starting to think that this whole religion and every other religion like it was a latched-on idea for people long ago

101

to calm themselves down whenever death came around," I said before scratching the back of my head. "I don't know. This Catholicism is just full of contradictions. I'd rather not be a part of it."

"Isn't your dad going to get mad?"

"He can't stop me from not going."

"You know, your dad doesn't have the forgiveness level that the god upstairs has?"

"Neither do I." My mouth was spilling things that I hadn't thought of. "But my relationship with my dad is probably not worth salvaging anyway." I looked at my reflection on the glass window and shot myself a look. *What the hell are you saying, Veo?*

"Why do you say that?" Val asked.

I sighed, trying to slow my thoughts down. I had to think carefully before I said anything to this cousin of mine. But as I regained control of myself, I realized that my dad hadn't been the best. All this proof of love that a parent should have for their kid was trash if they chose themselves over their kids. But that wasn't something I wanted to bring up to Val. "My brothers and I haven't seen our mom in a while."

"Oh, why not?"

"Money troubles."

"That's not all your dad's fault though, is it?" she said, raising a brow at me. "He's taking care of three boys."

There was no way to have her agree with me without telling her the truth. "He could do a better job," I said, cringing at myself for being an asshole.

She nodded, humming. "That's hot."

The rain let up, giving me a chance to escape with my

thoughts. Just as I was about to take a step out and say something, she opened her mouth. "Well, that's my cue. Here," she pulled out a marker and wrote on my forearm. "Text me whenever."

"I don't have a cell phone."

She backed up into the light rain before heading along her same route. "Then call me! We'll hang out soon."

I leaned against the wall once she was out of sight. I took a deep breath, feeling the space around me relax as I did. But what Val said repeated itself over and over again in my head.

That's not all your dad's fault though, is it? He's taking care of three boys.

MY BROTHERS AND I came home to find luggage laid out on the floor of the living room. I couldn't recall Dad saying that we were going anywhere. We hadn't been to Saipan in a long time, and I knew this probably wasn't it either. We were still struggling with money.

Matthew and Dominic's mouths dropped open when they entered behind me. But as they jumped around like happy Buddy whenever we came home, I called Dad out.

"Dad! Are you home?"

He came out from the corner, trying to hide the smile on his face. "*Umbiya*. Why aren't you guys packed for Saipan yet? We leave in seven hours!"

We all wondered if he had told us this before. I knew he hadn't. But when my brothers figured out that it was

Dad's surprise gift for us all, a bang of excitement pushed them to pack faster than they ever had before. Matthew and Dominic grabbed their luggage and ran for our bedroom as I stood there, considering the possibility that Dad was actually at church, listening to my conversation with Val, because it was such a strange coincidence. But that wasn't likely. The lawn outside smelled of freshly cut grass, and there was a plastic bag filled with mangos sitting on the kitchen counter. That took time for one person to do, so he couldn't have been at church. And it was something Dad would have us three do instead while he cooked lunch. Something was shifting in him.

I felt like my calves were switched out with heavy rocks, making it difficult to move them. There were words that my heart was putting into my mouth. But my mouth was the only one listening to my head that was telling it *Don't say it.*

"You okay, son?" Dad asked. His voice was still one that I didn't trust, but his tone softened my hold on the past.

My face stuck to its default as I locked eyes with him. No smile. No frown. No emotion. Blank.

He grabbed one of the suitcases, zipped it closed, and handed it to me. "Better get started. Your mom is waiting," he said before disappearing around the corner.

My thumb rubbed against the handle of my luggage. It was the same one I would have used years ago when he canceled the trip to Saipan. When I heard the door to his bedroom click shut, the argument between my head and my heart ceased as my mouth moved with a whisper so low that I knew he wouldn't be able to hear it even if he were in the room.

"Thanks, Dad."

"VEO! DOMINIC! MATTHEW! Come here, my boys!" Mom yelled across the pick-up zone. Her arms flew to us three, but unlike all the other times that I saw my mom, her arms varied by height. I was rolling my eyes as she kissed us all before we took off in her car for her place.

Dad sat in the passenger seat with Mom driving.

"How was the flight, Dan?" she asked.

"Eh. It was kind of rocky. Not the best plane ride."

"Are you tired?"

"What time is it?" Dad reached over to see the time on the dashboard. "It's what? It's 12:00 a.m.? Huh, I wonder why I'm so tired."

Mom pushed him back, laughing. Again, I rolled my eyes. We quickly got to her place in Chalan Kanoa. My brothers and I were tired, so once we settled in, we were knocked out for the night.

That night though, I had a dream, the kind that you remember when you wake up. We were back on Guam. Dominic, Matthew, and I were sitting on the couch with cops surrounding the house. I didn't know what was going on until Officer Frank approached us, telling everyone else to leave.

"Are you boys okay?" he asked. I looked over to my brothers to find them crying. Confused, I asked Officer Frank where our dad was.

"You guys are going to be living in nicer homes. Isn't that wonderful?"

Again, I asked where our dad was.

"Matthew? Matthew. Which one of you is Matthew?" the cop asked as he scanned the three of us. When nobody answered, he continued. "Matthew, you're going to live with Mr. and Mrs. Mantanona," He flipped through a binder, showing us all photos of an elderly couple. But Matthew wasn't entertaining the idea.

Officer Frank then showed us where Dominic's new home would be. But Dominic, like Matthew, wasn't entertaining it, with his eyes filling with tears fast.

I stood up and grabbed Officer Frank's wrist. "Sir, where is our dad?"

He finally came clean once he stood. "Your dad has been arrested for possession of drugs and is now deemed unable to take care of you boys." His stare was unwavering. "You won't be seeing him for a long time."

At that very second, I felt my shorts being grabbed with yelling behind me. I turned to find two other cops yanking my screaming brothers away, but Dominic held on to my shorts. I grasped his wrist, holding on to him as Matthew held on to Dominic.

"And Veo, you will be with Mrs. Smith. She is looking forward to having you. You might even be moving to her hometown in New Jersey."

My hold on Dominic was weak. I couldn't muster any strength no matter how much effort I put into it. It got worse as a hole formed in the back of the living room. The cop holding Matthew pulled him into the dark hole with ease. I heard Matthew's cries before he disappeared. "Matthew! No!" I screamed. But I had to stay strong.

I held on to Dominic even though no muscle in my body worked with me. I was managing to keep him here and I thought for a second that the cops were giving up. But then I felt short again, as short as I was before my growth spurt with my strength rapidly weakening to that of a cotton ball. Officer Frank grabbed the bottom of my legs, pulling me in the opposite direction of Dominic. I lost my grip on him fast. He slipped, hitting the floor, continuing to scream as he slid into the dark hole, instantly waking me up.

I shot up, panting, and fighting back tears I knew would stream out if I stayed in that dream any longer.

Matthew was sleeping on the couch, Dominic on the floor next to me, and Dad was on the two-seater. There was this tiny Christmas tree that was lit by the corner of the room next to the sliding door. Everyone but Dad was asleep. He was reading something in the dark. I couldn't see what, but he put it away when he heard me wake up.

"Bad dream?" he asked.

I was holding back the tears, telling myself over and over again that it was only a dream and that it didn't happen. But when I got a hold of myself, I nodded. "Yeah. Just a dream."

He chuckled a bit, which oddly enough, settled me down. "Whatever it was, don't worry. You've got your whole family here tonight."

I looked at him. My body relaxed as I matched the smile on his face. "Yeah," I whispered. "We're all here tonight."

DREAMS DON'T NORMALLY affect me. I've had worse ones with zombies and aliens and all that stuff. But after that night, I kept looking to Dad to say something for assurance. I don't know about what, but something. I needed to hear something from him.

"We're going to get firewood," he told us as he led us to some jungle area after a car ride in the early morning. The sun was peeking over the trees from where I saw. We took my mom's car, heading farther south of the island. When we got down with machetes, green stretched out for a distance beyond the road. We followed Dad as he walked through the tall green and made it to the trees. From there, we chopped up lots of wood.

"Why don't we get charcoal instead?" Dominic asked, sweating, and breathing hard.

"Barbecuing with wood tastes better than barbecuing with charcoal."

The conversation went on when I picked up long pieces of wood Dominic chopped up. I brought them to Matthew to cut into smaller pieces. My mind was going into robot mode, shutting off any thoughtful ideas. I did things without thinking. It's in that stage that I usually mess up, and that I did.

Dad was still talking about something when I turned around, felt a hard bump that I figured was a tree, and walked toward Matthew. It didn't occur to me that Dad stopped talking until I saw Matthew holding in his laughter. I put the wood down and looked back.

"Oy. Yeah, let's all hit Dad today," Dad said, rubbing the back of his head, his face pained and mouth hanging open. I couldn't help but laugh once Matthew started. I walked back to Dad and apologized, but he shrugged the pain off and took it, the same way he took pain when I was a child. Like a superman.

WHEN WE WERE heading back to Mom's place, I couldn't help but look over at what everyone was doing in the car. Matthew was playing with the radio, talking to Dad about island music with the accent he picked up whenever he was on Saipan. Dad was driving, listening to Matthew go on and on about island music. Dominic was sitting on the right side of the backseat, looking at all the places he could see from his side of the car. All seemed right with the world until I heard police sirens from behind us.

I didn't panic, but I heard muttering from Dad as he pulled over. I didn't know what he did wrong. He was driving well, so I couldn't help but think this had something to do with something else. Something nobody could have known here on Saipan.

My brothers and I listened and watched as he talked to the cop, who asked for Dad to step out of the vehicle. My thoughts wandered to the possible outcomes of this situation. Was this how my dream was supposed to start out? Was the dream a sign of what was to come? I glanced over to my brothers, hoping it wasn't. And I looked at my dad, hoping that he didn't stupidly get caught doing it again. If a child could find him doing drugs, it was clear he wasn't hiding it well.

I felt my inner self growl at the thoughts. My grudge toward him was resurfacing, reminding myself of why I talked back to him. I felt myself become the adult in the car as I watched Dad listen to the cop. I felt the stress in my head. But then it disappeared once I saw him shake hands with the cop, both of them smiling.

When he came back into the car, he told us that he ran a red light. But a talk with the cop on how early it was in the morning somehow got them onto the topic of who they knew on the island.

"Good. I was scared that you were going to get arrested," Matthew said as he sat back, folding his arms.

"I thought you were too. I didn't even see that traffic light," Dominic agreed.

"Don't worry, boys," he said. "I won't let that happen to you."

My eyes looked to Dad's in the backseat mirror as he started the engine. The radio played the island version of "Little Danny Grow" as Dad pulled back onto the road. But I kept my eyes on him, studying him. Dad glanced back at me with a smile and a soft look in his eyes that told me he was trying to be the dad I needed. We had hit a pothole, shifting his eyes back onto the road with a nervous laugh that planted a grin on my face, giving me what I needed to face the window. I relaxed. I finally relaxed as I watched the world go by with my dad in the driver's seat.

TRACK #8
Dominic

When I was 21 years old. . .

MOM PAID US a visit on Guam. It was also the last time I'd heard this song as it played on the TV while I waited outside for her. The guitar strumming that made up the song along with the singing was much better when played live. But I still appreciated the rhythm. I always bobbed my head to its pacing.

I was sitting on the steps when Dominic pulled in with Mom in the passenger seat. I was paying more attention to the vines on the mango tree. The vines looked like brown and gray wires suffocating the tree. They weren't there years ago.

"*Ai*, my Veo! Come here!" Mom threw her arms up in the air and over me. "How are you, my boy?" she asked, which went unanswered because Matthew stuck his head out of the screen door. He stole her away from me before I opened my mouth.

"Oh, my Matthew! Are you okay?" she asked him as I laughed with Dominic in the back. It didn't take long for Dad to respond to Mom's loud voice. His footsteps on the hollow floor of the house were fast as he came to greet her. But when he stepped out, Mom saw his posture had changed since the last time. His back slumped over enough for her to notice that he was in some pain. But he wasn't going to admit it.

"Oy, Joan. You said you were coming over tonight."

"Early appearance," she answered before gesturing for him to sit on the couch, which he fought. Dad had this motto: "The guest must sit comfortably before the residents sit at all." Something about etiquette.

Everyone eventually got comfortable though. Once she and Dad got settled in, she talked about the differences in the house from the last time she visited. She hadn't been here in a while. "I can see you painted the whole living room since then, Dan."

"Yeah, it needed touching up."

"So you painted the whole living room another color?"

Dad laughed with her before going on about how the house has changed. It wasn't long until the conversation dropped to more somber topics.

Mom had this thing about approaching serious matters in person as bluntly as possible. It was something Dad didn't respond to well, but they talked as if they knew how to handle each other.

"So, Dan, how are you feeling?" she asked.

"I'm good, Joan. Just a little sick, but I have time." Dad nodded. It wasn't long until everyone felt the room's energy dying because of his words. "It's been a long time since you've been here," he said, trying to pick up the mood.

"It has," Mom agreed, trying to force a smile. "When was the last time?"

"Five or six years ago, I think," Matthew chimed in. "When Veo had his first girlfriend, si Celestine."

At that point, everyone tried to remember the details of that weekend. But Dad turned to the person who would remember that time best: me.

"I'm pretty sure anyone here could tell the story of that weekend, Dad," I argued.

"Well, I want to hear it from you, boy. Tell it," he said.

Before I started, I opened the door to those memories that I didn't reflect much on. But I did start.

"I was a freshman the last time you came over, Mom. Celestine was my first girlfriend who I'm sure I told you about. The Friday that you came over, I was waiting for school to be over, so I could see her."

FIFTEEN-YEAR-OLD ME WAS sitting in class, bored out of my mind. English. I didn't think it was useless. Why? Because everyone around me was still getting C's and D's on the simple questions of grammar. But since I was getting A's, did I really have to take it?

I looked up at the clock, waiting for the hands to strike the time when I could relieve myself of this class. Tick. Tock. Tick. Tock. I started clicking my tongue to the rhythm of the clock. Click. Click. Click. Click.

"Who is doing that?!" Ms. Aldrin spun around, already irritated. At the same time, the bell rang. She rubbed her forehead, letting out a breath of frustration. It must have been hard to teach English to people who thought they knew the language so well that they didn't listen. I laughed though. "Sorry, Ms. Aldrin!" I said with a grin that reached my ears as I jumped past everyone and out the door.

I ran out to the tree to see Celestine before she left. But no matter how fast I ran, I knew that I'd only see her for ten minutes at the most. I always wished that she'd stay back, that we'd hang out somewhere, but I already knew she would say something along the lines of "My parents are going to kill me if they find out about you" or "I need to study or else my parents will suspect that I have a boyfriend." She said these things with a lot more exaggeration than usual, but I thought nothing of it. My parents would have been okay if I started dating when I was a baby. My opinion on the matter meant nothing. It was best to keep my mouth sealed instead of wasting our ten minutes on that topic.

Seung and Ding were already standing under the tree, looking at their phones with smiles that anticipated laughter. Ding was probably showing him some funny videos. I caught my breath, hunched over, trying to collect myself to make it look like I hadn't been running all across campus just to see her.

"Where is it? Oh wait. Never mind. Celestine probably has it," said Seung.

"What? Where's what? Has what?" I asked, still trying to slow down my breathing.

"The whip for your ass."

"Ha. Ha. Ha," I mocked. "She wouldn't—"

"Hey Veo," I heard Celestine sing behind me. She had

this flirty tone of voice that she used with me that I liked. But I knew that Seung was rolling his eyes behind me.

Celestine didn't have the same level of excitement that she did the first week we were official (which was the week before). I didn't think she liked me any less though. But I thought that maybe I was annoying her, asking her if there was anything wrong or anything bothering her too many times. She always answered with a no. And it was reaching a point where her attention was fleeting, going to whatever else was on her mind. If she didn't want to talk about it, it was okay with me. Everyone had their ways of getting through something.

I met her eyes with anticipation as an idea struck me that could make her day.

"Hey Celestine. Have you ever tried Updog?" I asked, trying to hide my laughter. She pulled her head back and raised a brow.

"What's 'Updog'?" she asked.

"Nothing much. What's up with you?" I laughed. After a second, I stopped laughing to see if she was, but I only saw her brows coming together as she shook her head. "Clever," she replied with a straight face.

I nodded, embracing the thought that there would be some jokes she didn't like and some she did. This was one she didn't. But it was okay. I had all the time in the world to get to know her.

She took my hand and before rubbing it against her cheek the way she liked it, her bus honked. Her eyes lit up, like she wanted to escape me. But I was probably overthinking it.

"Oof! There's my bus. I best be going," she said before

locking me in an embrace. "Oh, and I have a surprise for you."

I felt my manliness decrease in size once I sang out, "Ooh. What is it?"

The snickering behind me pushed it even further down.

"Uh, it's a surprise. Weirdo. I'll give it to you on Monday? Lunch time?"

"Why don't you come over to my place tonight? My mom is actually staying for the weekend, so I'll be needing an excuse to—"

"On Monday," she interrupted, giggling. I watched her run to her bus. The uniforms weren't the sexiest things to wear, but she always wore it in a way that made me want to tear it apart, especially when she was having her moments in class. The kind of moments that made her shine because of her brain. I loved it when she said something I didn't know.

"Dude, Veo," Seung called with arms out.

I raised my palm at him. "Yeah, yeah, yeah." What was left of that conversation didn't go on until everyone else had left.

I was sitting on my bag when Seung tried to tell me that Celestine was bad news for me. "I heard some things about her, man."

"Like what?"

"Like she's playing with two different guys," he scratched the back of his head. "I don't know if it's true, but something is off with her."

"You're basing that off what you heard."

"No, I'm also basing it off how she is around you. You're all romantic and sappy, but she isn't."

"She was. But she has something going—"

"Fine. Fine," he interrupted, before dropping it completely. My bus honked, triggering a smile, a sign of relief that this was the end of that topic. But as I was walking away, I realized it was the same smile that Celestine had on her face.

I WAS STEPPING out of the bedroom when I heard the front screen door slam shut. Dad yelled, "We're picking your mom up in two hours!"

Buddy came up to me, wagging his furry blonde tail before returning to Dad. Once Dad saw me, he smiled. "Hey, son. How was your day?" he asked.

"It's fine."

"How's Celestine?" Dominic asked with his eyes glued to the TV.

"Who's Celestine?" Dad asked.

"It's the girl he's seeing," Dominic answered before I could even open my mouth.

Dad's surprised look had me cringing at the thought of talking about her. I shrugged it all off though. He looked like he was waiting for more, but I turned my attention to the TV. The sudden interest in my new girlfriend shouldn't be a surprise. I wanted everyone to shut up about her. I felt my skin start to boil as Dad continued waiting to hear more about her, but I kept my growing temper to myself. I got up and left the room, deciding to hide myself in the bedroom with the door closed and locked. It wasn't only my room, but I didn't care. Dad was the last person I'd talk to about Celestine even if she wanted to meet him.

I WOULDN'T SAY that I was dreading that weekend, but I was dreading the time with my parents. I was avoiding both of them.

On Saturday though, Mom was helping Dad with some project on the computer. I was out exploring the jungle with my brothers and Buddy, but my parents were in the same positions they were in when we came back. I called Celestine a couple of times that day, resulting in a busy line after it rang three or four times. I was about to call her again when I returned. But my mom assigned me clean-up duty with the kitchen, which was washing the many dishes used to cook the pot full of *sinigang*.

I sighed, dreading the dishes. It was the last chore I ever wanted to do. I'd rather mow the lawn or clean the bathroom. It was the gunk of soaked inedible food that sat on the drain, yelling for my attention, which I'd only give it when it blocked water from going down.

"Oy, boy, do the dishes. I'm not going to say it again," Mom exclaimed.

"He's just being a teenager, Joan."

"Doesn't matter. Go do it, Veo."

"I will," I said before I looked down on the pile of dishes. Crap. I wanted to get back at my mom somehow, so I took my shirt off and hugged her with my sweaty body. I rubbed my face on her neck, making her cringe.

"*AIIIIII!*" she yelled, laughing before she hit me with the rolled-up magazine that I didn't notice was in her hand.

When I let go, my mood changed. There was a smile on both our faces. I figured that it was the strange effect of human touch, so I shrugged it off.

By the looks of the computer screen, my mom was teaching my dad how to burn a CD. By this time, the CD was an already outdated way of getting music. But I played stupid as I asked her what they were doing on the computer.

"We're making your dad a CD to play in his car. Do you know how to do this? Can you do it?"

My dad turned to me. Something was telling me to let him figure it out for himself. Of course, I didn't want my mom to see that on my face. I turned my attention back to the screen, my silence serving as an answer.

My dad quickly got the message though. "Never mind. Never mind. You teach me, Joan," he said, growing impatient.

My eyes lingered on the list of songs he had written on a piece of paper. "'Dominic'," I read, triggering the guitar tune to sing in my head. "It's a good song."

Dad's guitar sat by the TV, and I walked over to try figuring the strumming pattern and chords out myself. Somehow, it didn't take me long. I was better at it than I was when I was a kid. But my mom wasn't around for that, and it was obvious.

"He's just like you, Dan," she commented. "He's so gifted with music."

I rolled my eyes, continuing to strum. *I'm nothing like him.*

SUNDAY WAS A beach day. Everyone, including Auntie Connie and Uncle Dun, headed down south before noon. I was lucky enough not to be assigned barbecue duty. That job fell to Dominic, who did pretty well. Such a good job actually that everyone was silent when they ate his stuff.

That day was so remarkable with the little details. It's an odd way to remember something, but it's how I remembered it. The sounds of the waves pulling in and out of the sand with Matthew pretending to water bend as if he were in the world of *Avatar: The Last Airbender*. The Hiragana symbols that Dominic and I drew in the sand as we tried to spell our own names and write words. The masks that sat on the shore while my brothers and cousins looked for them, because they didn't know how to *not* lose them. And the fishing lines Dad and Mom threw into the water, hoping to catch something. That day fell too fast into night when I wanted it to last awhile.

By the time night had hit, we only had one car, so Dad made several trips back and forth, which took a while. The beaches at night were incredibly dark. The pavilion was full of the sounds of *zories*, the island's plastic flip-flops, scraping the concrete floor sprinkled with sand. I could hear the plastic bags that crunched up whenever my mom tried to pack things into smaller amounts so we could save a trip. And I could hear the ice cubes hitting each other and water hitting the soil once the contents of the cooler were spilled out. All those sounds were in the dark. Eventually, I got bored of hearing those sounds though. So I lay out on the sand by the shore, listening to every small sound of nature and watching the clear night sky. I wasn't expecting anyone to find me, but my mom did.

She lay beside me. I heard her take a deep breath before I asked if she was okay.

"I'm great, son. I missed you and your brothers. I wish I could stay longer."

I stayed silent.

"But even if I did, I'd just be talking to your dad the whole time since you boys are in school."

"Yeah. I wouldn't want to miss school tomorrow anyway," I said.

"Oh yeah? That's good, Veo."

I'd always wondered about them. My parents. They got along well enough, better than any couple. They were good friends, so it came out of my mouth. "Mom, why aren't you with Dad?"

She sighed as I continued. "You guys rarely fight, and you get each other's jokes. You can sit in the same room and still find things to talk about. Why aren't you together?"

Her eyes were still in the night sky. "Because your grandma was sick. She's still sick. And your dad, well, he didn't want to move away. And your grandma, she didn't like it that your dad was a Guamanian anyway. It's a long story, son. Full of unnecessary drama that was out of my control. But you boys are alive and well, and your dad is too. Your grandma doesn't have that." I nodded. "You boys are always welcome to stay with me in Saipan, though."

My brows furrowed. "What?" It was a strange thought since I believed she was the one who sent me off to live with Dad. "Then why didn't you want to raise me when I was with you?"

She sat up and shot me a questionable look. "You think I didn't want to raise you?"

I didn't answer.

She had things flying in her mind, I could tell. "I didn't want to tell you this when you were a kid, but I think you're old enough to understand. There was a night that you walked into your Uncle Mike doing something. Ice. And because you looked up to him so highly as the only man around the house, I couldn't risk it. Having you around that stuff would break my heart."

I stared at her, piecing everything together until she rubbed my back. "Veo, I love you. I love you and your brothers. But your dad is the best one to raise you." Nodding, I realized that she didn't know what Dad did. It wasn't something she should know either. She was fighting her own battles while trying to be a good mom from miles away.

I smiled. I didn't need to know any more.

"Mom, I have someone." Although it was dark, I could hear her lips smacking, smiling, and waiting. "Her name is Celestine."

"Celestine," she repeated. "Lovely name. Tell me more."

And I did. I told her Celestine's likes, her dislikes, her intelligence, my competition with her on grades. And I told her the story of how we got together.

"Ey. Wow. You really like this girl, huh?"

I nodded, feeling the sand dig deeper into my scalp.

"You know, son, I'm proud of you."

It was an odd thing to say when talking about a new

girlfriend, so I couldn't help but ask her why even though it was nice to hear.

"Because you know what your first word was?" she asked.

I rolled my eyes, chuckling a bit. It was a story she always reminded me of even though I don't remember the exact moment of my first word. But I always let her tell me. "What was it, Mom?"

"Mooooon," she imitated little me. I could tell that she was still smiling in the dark. "We were back home. I came outside to you and your dad sitting on the hood of his pick-up. You weren't even a year old, my boy. But once your dad pointed to the moon and told you what it was, you pointed at it, and said it. 'Mooooon.'"

"Why are you so fascinated with that story, Mom?"

"Why shouldn't I be?" She waited for an answer, but I didn't know how to answer that, so she continued. "I tried to make you say 'Mama' a lot," she laughed. "Having your first word be something you like—and I mean, interests you, fascinates you, grabs hold of your attention so that you want to know more about it—at that young of an age, makes me know that you have a mind of your own. That you won't adapt to what everyone else is saying or doing because they're doing it. And I know that when the time comes, you'll be able to take care of yourself and your brothers."

I saw the moonlight in her eyes before I thanked her. She turned her eyes back to the moon and said, "Your dad is raising you right. Even if you don't think so, Veo, you're learning the lessons you need to learn."

I turned back to the moon, speechless. I had nothing to

say, because I disagreed. But it didn't matter until I heard her say the next four words that still ring in my ears now.

"And he is too."

THE NEXT DAY, I stood in the walkway at school for a while. I don't know how long I stood there. I lost sense of time. My stomach dipped as my chest ached. All the other students either stared at me, wondering what I was doing, or paid no attention to the still, stupid guy standing in the busy walkway. But I was stuck in my own world, staring off in one direction. The direction of her open classroom door.

It felt weird. My thoughts crowded with memories and moments of only her. There weren't many. We had only been dating for a week or two, damn it. But I couldn't think of anything else once I saw her planting a kiss on some guy before heading into their homeroom.

What the hell.

I SAT ON the school bus, trying to pay no mind to the others whose eyes were on me. But by lunch, I was the talk of the day, though I couldn't blame them.

Once the bell rang for lunch, I found Celestine waiting outside my classroom door. She had a content look on her face, proud even. She was standing there with a faithful demeanor and bright eyes, acting as if she hadn't done anything wrong, as if I didn't know. I rolled my eyes at her once I saw her. Her smile disappeared fast.

"What's wrong?" she asked. But I didn't answer.

The cafeteria wasn't far, but by the time I reached its doors, she was pulling at my uniform. "Baby, baby, I got my present for you. Don't you want it?"

At this point, there were only a few students around, but even if there was a whole crowd, I still would have done what I did.

"Baby, come on. Talk to me," she insisted.

"I was outside your fucking homeroom this morning!"

She finally shut up. Of course, she tried to hide it, but she didn't do it very well. "Really? I didn't see you."

"That's probably because I couldn't move since I saw you kissing your other boyfriend."

"What?" She attempted to laugh, but again, I saw right through her.

I wasn't having it. I pushed the door open, but she got a hold of my arm. All her words after were gibberish and quavering, and I wasn't having any of it.

"Leave me alone," I said, pulling away as I entered. But what followed was what caused the talk of the day.

"Veo!" she yelled. She sounded both desperate and angry, but I ignored her.

I continued walking until I heard a guy's voice shout at me. "Hey, man. What the hell! Take it outside, you asshole!"

I turned around to find that it was the guy she was kissing that morning. He was heading for me with his arms flexing and his fist held tight. The typical sight of a guy ready to fight. But I only scoffed and turned around.

"You're her ex that can't take a hint, huh?" he said.

"You probably can't take a hint either, asswipe," I said.

I turned around to look at Celestine who was just angry at this point. The whole cafeteria had quieted down to listen to the fight that appeared to be coming on. Celestine joined the guy at his side the guy and I walked toward them both.

"Asshole!" she yelled.

But again, I only scoffed. "If you think that you're worth fighting over, then you're not as smart as I thought you were," I told her. I turned to the guy and held out my hand. Confused, he took it and shook. "Keep her. I don't want her."

My mind shook off reliving that lunch as the bus stopped at my spot. I hadn't noticed that Dominic was sitting next to me until he got up. "Come on, Veo."

Once we got off the bus, he said, "Epic break-up." I glanced at him and saw he was holding back his laughter. That triggered a laugh in me that was uncalled for. It was the shift of the day that reminded me that school wasn't everything. Only my friends and brothers were.

We headed home to find Dad by the stove, cooking. Dominic told him what happened at school, and he nodded with this look of pride on his face. "Not bad," he said. I couldn't stop my laugh again.

Once Dad put a big bowl of chicken curry on the table, Dominic got up to get a plate. But Dad stopped him, telling him that we were eating this and whatever Auntie Connie was cooking at her place tonight. "So bring it up. And don't touch it yet."

Dominic groaned a little before heading out, though it

wasn't long until dinner. But I just sat on the couch. The house grew quiet once Dominic left, and I started feeling alone again. I knew I was about to get lost in my thoughts, and I probably would have let it if my dad didn't ask me if I was alright.

I nodded, fidgeting with the leather of the couch. "Yeah, I'm good."

Dad grabbed a plastic bag off the kitchen counter and sat at the other end of the couch. He took a deep breath and looked at me. "Even if you aren't, there are plenty of other mangos on the tree."

I nodded again, but I felt a smile on my face. It grew even bigger when he pushed the plastic bag on my lap and told me to pick some mangos for dinner tonight.

"AND THAT'S ALL I remember," I said, finishing off the story.

Dad groaned lightly, catching my attention since I knew how he sounded when he was in pain. It took a lot for him to make a sound. I got up to look for the right medication and Matthew and Dominic cleaned up as Mom and I helped Dad relax.

"You feeling any better, Dan?" Mom asked after covering him with a blanket.

"Yes. Thank you," he said.

"You know, I always thought that Matthew would be the one to go to a university," Mom said, to lighten the mood.

"Wow, thanks, Mom," Dominic said. Mom burst out

laughing before she went on saying how she expected him to build his own business instead of going to college.

"Really?"

"Yeah, my boy. You're very creative. You don't need to go to school to turn your creativity into success. But I'm proud of you either way!"

Like a bashful little cartoon character, Dominic snuggled up to her.

"Who do you think is going to have kids first then?" Matthew asked from the kitchen.

"You."

Everyone laughed, even Dad. Given how our lives were going before the news of Dad's condition, Matthew was probably the only one touching the whole "I want to start a family" idea with Kayla. He didn't even deny it. "It will be you. . . then Veo," Dad said.

"Pfft! Sorry to bust your bubble, but I'm never having kids."

"We'll see," Dad said.

"Who do you think will get married last then, Mom?" Matthew asked.

"Probably Veo."

I shrugged, agreeing. "Yeah. Probably me. If I ever get married at all."

"Well, if you did, that's something. . . I would want to see for myself," Dad said.

The air grew awkward at the thought, forcing Mom to leave the room. Matthew and Dominic proceeded to finish cleaning up the living room. As for me, I handed Dad his medication, but I looked away when his eyes met mine. It was the first time he had ever heard the reason Mom sent me to him all those years ago, along with my brothers. And it had to be followed up with talk of an event that he might not even go to.

The lines on his face were deepening. I knew what would follow would be something uncomfortable to talk about, so I stopped it from coming up.

"Want some water?"

He nodded before I went to get him a glass.

TRACK #9
A Man to the Sun

When I was 13 years old. . .

AFTER SCHOOL, I took the warmer way to the bus stop by crossing the field so I could defrost from staying inside an air-conditioned room all day. The synchronous voices of all the students grew louder as I took each step, my head telling my feet to keep stepping on the lines of the pavement. But once I heard a car honk, I looked up to find Matthew and Dad waving at me from beyond the fence. When I ran over, Dominic appeared not long after.

The drive over to where Dad wanted to take us took only two minutes. But when we got out, I wondered why he brought us here. It was the shopping center in Agana that needed a big update. Its walls needed a fresh coat of paint, and its doors needed to be replaced. The few windows that the building did have should have been multiplied by five or ten, because the place looked like a jail. It was a shopping center that had a few shops in them. About two or three sold food. Two or three provided services. And only one sold clothes. Everything else was offices that made up half the space of the building inside. It was boring.

As we stepped into the one-story building, the floor tiles and wall paints were already screaming at me to help them be pretty again. They were asking the wrong guy, though. The low lighting overhead stressed my eyes out. It would have helped if there was a window somewhere, but the only sunlight coming in was the little bits that entered from the tinted entrance door.

I looked over to my dad for the purpose of our visit, knowing there was a reason. There was a twinkle in his eyes and a smile planted across his face that made me curious.

When we reached a glass office door, he stopped. His eyes landed on us, looking the most excited that I ever saw him. I still hear his voice ringing in my mind before we entered. "Boys, we have our own business."

As we walked into his small office, I saw my brothers' faces. Their eyes beamed with support for him. But for me, it was an even bigger moment. It was the moment I put two pieces together. The piece where I realized that my dad was an independent thinker and worker, and that owning a business would be perfect for him to support the family. And the piece where I realized that my dad was putting all his effort into growing again, not only for himself but for us all. This was the moment where I thought he'd be shining from thereon, and it was marked by the song that was playing off his stereo system that sat by his metal desk.

The island stole my sanity, my mood, and let me
Speak solely to the sun for some hope

131

*But she kept whining and complaining, and she burned
me insane*
That I'd find comfort in the night when she's gone

TWO YEARS LATER, I was up on the roof, stargazing on a clear night when I heard the front screen door bang shut. I thought nothing of it though since I figured that one of my brothers would be coming up to join me. But I was wrong.

"Veo! GET DOWN HERE NOW!" Dad yelled from inside. My lips pursed as I felt my stomach brace for the scolding that was coming. I made my way down, saying goodbye to the stars for the night. Once I came in, I found him standing in the middle of the room with his back hunched over in exhaustion. If my brothers hadn't been sitting on the couch, he likely would have fallen onto its cushions and drowned in slumber. His face looked like it was trying to relax before he heard me coming in. But once he saw me, he gave up all effort and started scolding me for always costing him so much money because I tended to tamper and break things when I was up on the roof. Dad's little Walkman player, for example. Dominic's camera too. And my own leg at one point.

Matthew and Dominic went to bed. The scolding went on for a while, long enough that the words coming out of Dad's mouth weren't going in my ears anymore. They were floating around my head, ineffective at entering my brain.

My head deemed them useless and hollow for the night, like it did in school with boring subjects.

Eventually, his energy depleted, but his voice was firm as he told me to go to bed. I turned for the bedroom when I heard his movements behind me. He snarled as he searched for the blanket that was usually behind the couch. By the looks of it, he couldn't find it. He must have had a hard day to tire himself out this much.

I came back to tuck him in for the night after giving him the blanket. He'd finally shut his eyes for the day, his face furrowed. I watched him, making sure he had everything he needed.

IT WAS CAREER Day the next day. The auditorium was big, fitting the whole school with presenters and their little stands. It looked like a science fair with each student mingling with students from other classes, teachers, and presenters.

I walked around, finding the careers of teachers, barbers, police officers, firemen, lawyers, and so many others. But none of them piqued my interest until I turned the corner to the stand near the garbage bin. It wasn't like this career was trash. There were a few students asking the guy questions. But because he didn't bring any animals with him to reel in students' attention, they stayed away because of the smell from the nearby trash.

I headed for his stand as he talked to the principal. Once I was within arm's reach, I heard her apologizing to him repeatedly for the smell. The guy held up his palms with an assuring smile that even put me at ease. He spotted me as I was about to turn around because I didn't wish to interfere.

"Young man," the guy started. "Do you think it smells here?"

The principal turned to me as the guy mouthed "Say no."

And I did just that. "Nope. What smell? There's a smell in here?"

The principal and the guy laughed before she left him saying, "Well then, I'll leave you to the students."

"Nice save," he told me with his thumbs up. With his stance, he looked like an anime hero character, but I couldn't assume he watched cartoons at his age. My eyes crinkled as I held back a chuckle.

"So you interested in becoming a veterinarian, young man?"

I shrugged before I asked him to tell me more about it. What followed was information on two of the few things in school that interested me. Science and animals. He handed me a pamphlet before telling me his name, Dr. Cabrera.

"Veo Mafnas," I told him as I shook his hand. Before we parted, he invited me to visit his clinic. Whenever I felt the need to start with my journey on to becoming a vet, I was welcomed. All I could do was thank him at that point, because at the time, I didn't know what I wanted to be. A vet sounded cool, but the idea of becoming an astronaut was making its appearance again in my dreams.

As I walked away, the bell rang, and the principal alerted us that school was ending. I didn't realize that it was noon already. But since everyone had their mesh bags, I headed for the bus area.

"Hey! Veo! Wait for me!" I heard Dominic calling from behind. He tried to keep calm as he told me that one of the presenters was a filmmaker. It was an area that I knew Dominic had tried messing around with, but I didn't think he'd like it that much. I saw the smile dancing on his lips that he tried to hide as we walked. He told me that the filmmaker he met won awards for his film, and that he had idea after idea.

"But he also said that 'Things don't always work out the way you want it to.' I don't know, man. He sounded like a real person, but he's doing such great work."

"You want to be like that?" I asked, curiously.

He shrugged, smothering the child-like attitude I knew he thought he was showing.

"It's okay if you want to be like that."

He looked at me, smiling. He nodded as his beaming eyes dropped to the ground. "Yeah, I want to be like that."

I pulled his neck in and messed up his hair, forcing him to laugh. He pulled away, shaking his hair loose.

"Then you'll be like that," I told him, knowing that he could do great things.

DOMINIC AND I got home around 1:00 p.m. Matthew was sitting on one of the chairs in the garage with his leg shaking and his chin propped against his hand. He didn't seem to notice us coming in until I stood right in front of him. Even then, he only took a deep breath.

I asked him if he was okay, but he couldn't seem to answer. He stood up and tried to make a noise, but he couldn't.

The front screen door opened and shut, and I found Uncle Dun there. "Come inside."

We all went inside and sat on the couch once we were told to. Just like ripping a bandage off, Uncle Dun said it. "Your dad is in the hospital."

Suddenly, there was something in my throat, halting the noise in me. I couldn't speak. I felt a nervous feeling in my gut as I listened to Dominic asking what happened.

"He got into an accident with the pick-up."

"Is he going to be okay?"

Uncle Dun didn't answer. We all knew that he didn't know.

"Well, what happened? Was he hit by another car? Was he wearing his seat belt? What happened?" Dominic asked.

"I'm not sure. The police said that he ran a traffic light, and an incoming car hit the passenger's side of the pick-up, but your dad wasn't wearing his seat belt. He hit his head on the window."

"That's impossible," started Matthew. "He always rolls down the windows. The air-con doesn't work in there."

"Well, he must have kept them up this time."

I felt my heart beating out of my chest, as I stopped listening. I wished it were the night before, having my dad yell at me instead of all this arguing if he was going to make it. But I shook it off. That wishful thinking wasn't going to get me anywhere. I stood up as they continued talking and headed for my dad's room, but as I made my way there, I heard his playlist playing a song with a familiar scent in the air. It was a scent that I hoped I never got to smell again. But I opened his bedroom door, finding the same stuff he had used years ago. It was laid out the same way as before. I stood there, feeling like I was eleven years old again with the track playing in the room.

She knows about my journey and my past and my pain
It felt good to be away from the sun
But I woke up to her slap of heat, her cursing my name
I'll soon die with a head gone insane

BY 5:00 P.M., I had hidden away the things that I found in my dad's room. I couldn't tell if I was angry or hopeful. It was a mix of feelings that I hated to be put through, and as I thought of this mix of feelings, I grew even angrier. I wished to bring him to consciousness so I could curse him out for even making me feel this way. I wished I could have told him every bad thing ever said. But I didn't know if he'd be alive by the end of the day or if he was even alive then. I couldn't wish for him to die, so I sat on the chair with my brothers and Uncle Dun in the hospital waiting room, dwelling on my angry thoughts and hoping that he'd still be alive.

I must have had my eyes on the ground for so long because Matthew patted me on the back. "It's going to be fine," he whispered with his eyes straight ahead. I hadn't noticed that his posture was upright with his face as serious as could be. He must have assumed the leadership role while my eyes were elsewhere. It was a funny role Matthew was playing, but now wasn't the time to laugh.

"Yeah, it is," I said in a low voice.

A nurse popped out from a corner, holding a clipboard, and called out for Uncle Dun. My brothers and I watched as he went up to talk to her. When he turned around, I saw the corners of his mouth turn up as he called us over. We followed him and the nurse to Dad's room. On the way, I couldn't decide what to feel. But that all changed once I saw Officer Frank come out of the room we were heading to. For a second, I worried about him bringing my dad to jail, but his face was calm. There was even a hint of a smile as he greeted Uncle Dun. And once Uncle Dun told us to amen him because he too was our uncle, it all clicked in a second. The pipe, the accident, this hospital, and Officer Frank, the supposed advocate for a drug-free community. Dad could do anything he wanted to fucking do, and he wouldn't be going to jail. I remember him telling me the same crap everyone else on this island believed—that it's all about who you know.

Once we got to his room, I saw Dad move his head. My brothers stood at his bedside in an instant with Uncle Dun standing at the foot of the bed. A conversation went on between the four on my dad's condition as I stood by the door. I was observing my family and felt further away than ever before. What should I have done? I didn't know.

My dad spotted me by the door and called me over, but I shook my head.

"And why not, son? Come, give me a hug."

"My bladder is about to explode," I lied as nonchalantly as possible, taking a step back, trying to suppress my angry thoughts from building up. But Dad knew I was lying since I wasn't rushing into the bathroom behind Uncle Dun that everyone else was telling me to go in.

My eyes dropped to the ground. "I'm going to another restroom, Dad. It looks dirty."

I turned around to stop the conversation from continuing. What he said next held the most disappointment he ever had in a voice. Whether that disappointment was in me or him, I couldn't tell. And I was getting to a point where I didn't care anymore.

I opened the door, ready to roam the halls of the hospital when he said it.

"Okay, son. There's another one down the hall."

TRACK #10
Livin' it up in Mexico

When I was 16 years old. . .

FOR THE WEEK and a half that my dad was in the hospital, my brothers and I visited him every day after school. Sometimes Uncle Dun would drive us there. Sometimes, it was Auntie Connie. Funny thing was that his stuff still sat in the far hidden corner of the uppermost shelf in the closet of his room. You could argue with me that it was his pick-up truck that got him into the hospital, but I knew very well that that wasn't it. And every time I thought about throwing away the stuff that got him to where he was now, my head would boil with thoughts that would only go away once I forced myself to forget about it all.

But the day before Dad's discharge, Auntie Connie came by the house, dangling her car keys and yelling through the house for us to get ready quicker. Dominic was stuck in the bathroom, especially after a bus ride full of him clutching his gut and groaning from needing to let out a number two. Matthew was sorting through our bedroom closet for a change of clothes. And I was in my

140

dad's bedroom, feeling the heat rise again in me as I stared at his shut closet.

"Let's go, boys! I'm leaving with or without you in ten minutes!" Auntie Connie yelled as she banged the front screen door.

I walked out and told her that I needed to stay to catch up with homework.

"You can do your homework when we get there. Just grab your things and let's go," she said with only half of her attention on me.

"Auntie Connie," I said as straightforward as I could, "It's distracting, and I'm behind."

She gave me a frosty look before scrutinizing the situation. "Okay, Veo. Don't be going anywhere. Stay here at home. I better not hear about you going to the store just because you're hungry."

I nodded, and in what felt like a minute, she and my brothers jumped in her car, driving off to see Dad. But what followed were a bunch of stupid decisions made in haste all because I felt like I was too familiar with how to get rid of this stuff. Before I knew it, I was sitting on the backseat of a police car, catching sight of the grinning Joseph Reyes observing everything from his fenced lawn across the street.

I DON'T REMEMBER much of this part of my life, because I tried to block it out. But what I do remember was sitting in what looked to be an old office for what felt to be days.

Getting arrested wasn't as scary as I pinned it to be. I wasn't a druggie, so this stuff was easy to "let go of." My focus wasn't on my situation. It was on my brothers.

I imagined Dominic sitting on the edge of the couch with his arms crossed over his chest. He wouldn't look mad, but you could tell that there was something going on in his head. Nothing surrounding him would sink into his brain. Not even the strong punch and kick sounds from *Tekken 5* that Matthew usually played from the other couch. The excitement on Matthew's face would go haywire if he were losing against the computer, eventually resulting in him smashing each button as if it helped him win. But in my head, he wouldn't be his usual self. Matthew would sink back into the cushions of the couch. His face would be as dull as his number two pencils—the teachers let you use pens in the sixth grade.

As for my dad, I couldn't tell what he would do. Would he be happy cooking dinner for the three people living in the house? Or would he be trying to cheer my brothers up with some advice? He'd be an asshole if he did. But I sat there, hoping that he would be sitting by the computer table, trying to soak in the reality that one of his sons got caught with his stuff.

UNCLE DUN AND my dad picked me up. The funny thing was that my dad didn't say anything. He didn't ask anything either. He was quiet as I sat in the back of Uncle Dun's sedan listening to the song playing on his CD player.

Livin' it up in Mexico
Drink it up, play it up
Dance, dance, dance
Live it up in Mexico
You wouldn't leave it
If you gave it a chance

"So Veo, how was jail?" Uncle Dun asked with smile. My dad hit his arm with the back of his hand before I felt my expression soften.

"It was fun. I—"

"Oy, don't be going back to jail now, boy," said Dad.

"Hey, Daniel. Your boy's not like that. He's a lot smarter than you give him credit for."

I glanced at Uncle Dun in the mirror, finding his eyes jumping from the road to my dad for a bit. A silent conversation between them? I couldn't tell.

"It probably wasn't even his," Uncle Dun said. "But it doesn't matter. That's all in the past. You still have those treatment sessions to attend to, but you're lucky your dad knows a guy. Veo, no more of that stuff, okay? Today will be a good day."

My dad agreed. "Matthew and Dominic missed you."

I felt the car hit grass and rocks. We were home already. As we drove further in, I saw Matthew and Dominic getting up from the steps by the front screen door.

Dominic was already by the window within seconds. He splattered his tongue and lips all over the backseat window. "WAM!" His face looked like cartoons did when they had hit a window seconds before sliding down the window.

It wasn't funny, but it was an attempt at something, anything to not remember what had happened to me. I remember the curve of his mouth rising once he saw me smiling. Stupidly pleasant brother stuff.

I got out to find Matthew heading for me. He sniffed at my shirt that I had worn the day I sat in the back of a police car, and he pulled back instantly with disgust. No sound came out of his mouth. His face said it all. Whether or not he was joking, I started calling him a dog. "Hey! That's one thing you could do. A police dog. Sniff out crime!"

Dominic pulled his head back in laughter. The jokes were coming out of us two faster than Matthew's attempt to joke about my scent until he finally turned around. He scrunched his cheek and waved his hand down saying, "Ahhh, whatever. Welcome home, bro." His way of losing.

We all went into the house and went about the day as if I had never left. Dad cooked up dinner before heading outside for the garage. It was almost time to watch the sunset with Uncle Dun while yammering on about politics that they disagreed on half the time. All the rooms in the house looked and smelled the same. Old wood. And my brothers had their eyes glued onto the TV, figuring out how to play *Tekken 5*. The video games were more fun than I remembered. While I lost half of the time, I didn't jam the same button over and over again like they did. Dominic, though, was catching on. By the late afternoon, he was skillfully playing his character. I had to admit I was jealous for a second. But I pinned that as a useless emotion and told myself to learn my character.

"A-ha-ha-ha!" Matthew was gleaming after winning a match. Dominic reacted unusually though. His face was indifferent, relaxed, and calm, but also somehow bored as he watched Matthew laugh at his loss.

"Oh, oh! Dominic doesn't care if he loses anymore," Matthew teased before the next round started. His laughs were loud but dwindled to silence as the tide turned the next round. I couldn't help but laugh until the next match began and ended with the same result. And then, the same result. And then, again.

"PLAYER TWO WINS!" the TV sang out for the fourth time. Matthew scratched his head before tossing his controller to me.

"Ey um, Veo, can I ask you something?" he asked, changing the subject of the night.

"Yeah, bro. What's up?"

"How was that stuff?"

"What stuff?"

"You know," he answered. He gestured with a long sniff followed by the corners of his mouth curving.

Before I even thought out if I should entertain being truthful about the background, I said it. Things would probably have turned out different if I didn't say it, but I did. "That stuff isn't so great to do. It feels terrible."

"Yeah, yeah, yeah. Because we're not supposed to do drugs, but—"

"The side effects are horrible, man. Why would you want to do that?"

"You're doing it."

"Not anymore," I lied, trying to glue my attention onto the TV. I tried to push this off as nothing, but his interest into that stuff was too concerning. I replayed the conversation in my head, finding out that I sounded like a cop advertisement for safety. I sounded like the kind of thing people hear way too often that it becomes background noise. *Don't do it. It isn't good for you.*

Matthew sat back, muttering something. I thought I caught what he was saying, but it didn't sound right to me. "What?" I asked as I pulled back a look.

"Nothing. I'll just get it from a friend."

I felt a panic. My brain short-circuited as my legs grew numb and warm. What followed was a burst of loud statements that I don't even remember saying. But it was loud enough for Dominic to pause the game and for both Uncle Dun and my dad to come in.

"Hey, hey, hey! Calm down! What are you getting so mad about?" my dad asked. But I stood there in silence, feeling my fists bunched up at my sides and my forehead stressed with my cheeks hot. I was angry, and I didn't know I got to this point.

"Don't want to say anything? Fine. Veo, go outside. Cool off. Hit a tree if you need to, but don't be bringing it here today!"

My body was doing before I was thinking, and I heard the screen door slam shut behind me as I walked to the darkening lawn. I paced back and forth until I blended in the night.

"Veo, what's been going on?" I spun around to find Uncle Dun standing by his car. I took a deep breath and said, "Nothing. I'm fine."

He didn't say anything. But I knew he was waiting for a longer answer, something he'd consider the truth. That wasn't something I was entertaining though. I only needed to calm down. I pulled myself together and stared up at the night sky. There were a few clouds overhead as I counted the stars I could see, which were many. *One. Two. Three. Four. . .*

"It's going to mess you up if you keep it in."

Five. Six. Seven. Eight. Nine. Ten. Eleven. . .

"Fine, Veo. But at this rate, you're only going to fall back into—"

"Back into what?"

"Back into—"

"Because I swear, I'm not doing it," I confessed. Once I realized what came out of my mouth, I paced faster. My pulse was racing. I knew that I shouldn't have said that.

"Then whose was it, Veo?" he asked as I continued pacing. I wished that I could have told him. I wished that I had someone to tell this to. But telling him? He was still drinking when his family left him.

Nobody was going to help me if everyone knew it was my dad's stuff. Matthew would welcome that crap even more to his life. He'd fall down a ditch that he'd keep digging to nowhere, making it even harder to get back up out of it. And Dominic, he could lose his chance at going to film school or traveling or whatever it was that he wanted. I couldn't do that to them.

"Veo, whose was it then? You gotta come clean about what you're responsible for, otherw—"

"Oh yeah, Uncle Dun? Then what are you responsible for?"

"What? We're not talking about me—"

I interrupted him, asking for his phone. "No, Veo.

You're not getting out of talki—" He stopped once I reached for his pockets. He fought me, but I managed to get his cell phone before running across the street. I dialed the three digits, giving them the information they needed to find me. "There are drugs. Uh, uh, meth. There's meth at my house, and I need help. Please send help."

I hung up the phone before Uncle Dun reached me. "Who did you call, boy? You had better talk."

I didn't say anything. There was no one who could help me. I didn't want things to change, but I also did. My arms were numb with anger as I felt my tear ducts being pressed. I fought back the tears. *Fuck. Fuck. Fuck.*

I was all alone.

"Who was it, boy?"

"Nobody," I lied, but he grabbed my wrist.

"I never pinned you down for a liar, Veo. Who. Did. You. Call."

I yanked myself from his grip, and stormed back inside the house, heading straight for the bedroom until I heard my dad say, "Are you cooled down now?"

Once he knew I wasn't answering, he called out my name, growing furious at my silence. "Veo! COME BACK HERE!"

He got up and ran to block my way to the bedroom. "Go back outside, Veo. NOW!"

"No."

"Now."

"No," I said again, and I felt the bad courage leading me up to continuing to say, "Get the hell out of my way."

"Veo! What the hell is your problem?"

Police sirens were sounding and growing louder and louder. Uncle Dun came inside, "You called the cops, Veo?"

"Get the hell out of my way!" At that point, we kept arguing back and forth until I heard Matthew yell at me to shut up. I stopped talking to find myself and my dad standing in the middle of the living room. I looked straight into Matthew's eyes.

"Veo, you don't talk to Dad like this. He's done so much—"

"Oh bullsh—"

"Shut up, Veo! He's a good dad whether you like it or no—"

"NO, HE'S NOT!" I finally cried out. What followed were tears streaming down my face, looking at everyone in the room as they saw me break down. "No, he's not! He's not a good dad. He's not!"

I scanned the room for anyone who could believe me, but I knew I was all alone on this too. I looked out at the blue and red flashing lights, wondering what to do next.

The room was silent. I didn't know what to say anymore. I didn't know what to do. So it didn't matter if anyone said anything to me afterward.

"Mr. Veo Mafnas?" a cop called out from the steps outside.

I turned around and held up my hand. "Yeah, that's me."

"Can we speak in private?" he said. Before I went outside, I looked back at my dad, whose face remained as calm as ever. It was a trait that easily made him a superhero to me when I was a kid. But I knew his heart was racing.

I nodded and left the house but came back after a stern

scolding about misuse of the police calls. Everyone stayed quiet as I made my way to the bedroom. My head was spinning and vibrating with a headache, so I went into my dad's room first. Before I fixed myself up to go into the right bedroom, I noticed Dad had put a cork board up in his room, attaching different papers onto it. But on the front of it all was a small torn piece of paper, written in big, bold letters: FOR MY BOYS.

At this point, I could only shake my head. I left his room and locked myself in the bedroom I shared with my brothers. I slept it off, hoping that maybe this was all just a bad dream.

TRACK #11
Leave It in the Dark

When I was 16 years old. . .

I DIDN'T TALK much to Seung and Ding and the whole gang. We'd usually set up sleepovers to finish a video game or film a project for school over the weekends. But ever since that night with the cops and Matthew asking for something, I didn't feel like talking to them. I didn't feel like talking to my brothers or my dad either.

I hung out with Val and her group at lunch, but the rest of the time during school, I kept to myself.

There was one day, before lunch, that my geometry teacher gave the class an early recess as a Friday celebration. I sat in the back, continuing a drawing that I'd started during his lecture when Seung approached me. "Hey man, I haven't seen you in a while."

I glanced up at him, but my eyes quickly latched back onto the piece of paper in front of me as I returned his greeting. I wasn't paying much attention to what he was saying. It probably was about the hang-out for the weekend, which I was sure of it when he put his hand on top of my drawing. "So are we still on for tomorrow?"

"What?"

"Tomorrow, Ypao Beach? You bring the grill? Remember?"

"Oh. Right, right. . ."

"It's somebody's birthday tomorrow."

I've always been so bad with dates, but it was a good thing that the date was always written on the whiteboard. October 26. The only one in our group who had his birthday in October was Seung. "Right. Right. Sorry man, I have a lot on my mind right now."

"It's cool." He glanced out the window with something on his mind. "But we're still doing tomorrow, yeah?" he asked.

I nodded. "Of course."

Some thanks came out of his mouth before he turned. But whatever was on his mind bugged him enough to pull up a chair in front of my desk. "Veo, man, what's up with you?"

My brow raised as I waited.

"Those juniors you've been talking to, they're bad news."

I sneered, about to say something, but I must have ticked him off already when he continued. "Look, I know you don't have much planned for after high school. But at least graduate without a drug addiction or a fucking baby."

The bell rang for lunch as he stood up and walked away.

VAL AND ZENA were talking during lunch about Zena's last night "hang-out" with Frankie. They went out to the theaters to watch *Saw V*. But they managed to skip out on the actual watching, which I guess, struck me as unfathomable. If either one of them was hoping to do something with the other, a movie that you try to solve before the ending hits is not the type of movie to see. There'd be a high chance of your eyes locking on the screen, wanting to know what happened next. Other than that, the movie is gory. If you managed to get turned on with that type of movie playing, then you've got a fetish or fantasy in the works there.

"Veo," Zena called. "Do you think he would want to do that again? He's been avoiding me all day. I mean, yeah, his girlfriend is in his class, but he could have said 'Hi' if he really wanted me."

I raised a brow.

"Oh, whatever. Like you're such an angel," she said, rolling her eyes. "I bet you've done all the girls in your village and all the girls in all your classes. Ugh. Men."

I shook my head. "Nope. Haven't been with a girl," I said. Val shot a surprised look at me. For a second, I thought that she was going to talk to me like she did before with that flirty tone in her voice, but she didn't. Even if she had, I had grown up enough to surpass my hormones that told me to reproduce with any available girl that came on to me. So sure, Val was still attractive, but that cousin aspect of our relationship killed whatever invitation she would throw my way. Sorry, Val. Well, kind of, not really.

"What? Didn't you go out with Celestine? Hasn't she been with several guys from our grade?" Zena asked.

She and Val went on, talking about her until Camille reached our table. Camille had long, black hair that was so well-taken care of that she might as well be considered a mermaid. Her skin was clear of blemishes, and her lips were full even when she smiled. But none of that compared to her ample ass. It would pull anyone's attention, especially when she wore shorts outside of school. I was lucky enough not to see it through the uniform, because if I did, I'd be staring.

"Veo?" Camille grinned as she called me out. "You okay?"

Val laughed, saying, "Yeah. You're staring again, Veo."

I apologized, looking down. If my skin was lighter, everyone would have seen all the blood in my body rush to my face. But there was a coquettish spark in Camille's eyes as she sat next to me, filling me up with more nerves than before.

"So how's it going, Veo? How are you?" she asked slowly. From the sounds of it, Val and Zena continued talking about other things and people. Although it was exciting to have someone as sexy as Camille talk and smile at me, I was drowning in nerves. I was trying to grab the topic of the nearby conversation but was failing badly.

She scooted closer to me. Her proximity made my vision blur and I scooted away only to land on the ground with my hands yanking my tray of food and spilling on my shirt. Embarrassed, yet again.

Camille helped me up. Her flirtatious attitude was out the door as I stood. "What size are you? I have an extra shirt in my bag. Let me get it!" she said before she ran out of the cafeteria before I answered.

I glanced over at Val and Zena, who were both holding back some laughs.

"Yeah, yeah, yeah. . ." I muttered.

Their laughs burst out, eventually pushing me out of my embarrassing state and joining them in their gleeful moment.

"But hey, I think she likes you," Zena said after she calmed down.

"Isn't she seeing Noah?" Val asked, but Zena shook her head. "Just broke up last night."

"They're always on and off though. They break up, they get together, they break up, they get together. It's like they're—"

"Eh, whatever. Go for it, Veo. She's a pretty girl," Zena said before Camille came back with nothing in her hands but her mesh bag.

"No extra shirt?" I asked, pulling everything I had to smile confidently at her. She tossed her hand in the air before turning to Val and Zena. They talked something over that I couldn't hear, but Val and Zena's eyes lit up with excitement.

Camille turned back to me. "Wanna go to the mall? I could get you a shirt over there."

"Oh, uh," I paused, thinking she forgot that my shirt was uncomfortably wet with stuff rats would love to feast off. It was a weird time to be asking me if I wanted to go to the mall after school too. "It's okay. This will dry by the time school ends."

"No, I mean, like, right now, we go."

"And skip school?"

Camille grinned at me. "You never skipped school or what?"

"Hey, at least break one virginity today, Mafnas!" Zena shouted. I felt a lot of eyes on me. So before Camille could ask, I asked her if we'd be taking her car.

WE ROAMED AROUND the mall for a bit before Camille bought a shirt for me. She was about to let me choose before she winked at me and decided that she'd choose how to dress me up for the rest of the day. I normally didn't care what I wore, but I admit that I was cringing at her choice. It was a tight black t-shirt with big font, reading "FBI: Female Body Inspector." But it was either that or the uncomfortably wet uniform top. I went with the dry shirt.

To say that I had never skipped school would be ridiculous. Everyone skips school at least once. For me, it was on the days where I wanted to finish *Devil May Cry 4,* so I'd pretend that I was sick. But to skip school to go to the mall earlier was something I wouldn't have tried to accomplish. The stores would still be selling the same stuff by the time you got there after school.

In this case though, I did it. And yes, it was to ensure that I wouldn't further embarrass myself in front of a hot girl.

By 3:00 p.m., we were sitting in the food court. Val, Zena, and Camille were conversing about some work-out program until Zena asked me what I did to exercise.

I shrugged, saying, "I just stick to PE. I don't really pursue fitness."

"Really? Because you look pretty muscular in that shirt," Zena said, her tone a bit too friendly.

"It's a stupid shirt that tourists wear," Val said, making Camille laugh and agree.

My hands flew up as I laughed, trying to mask my irritation. "What? Oh my god. Then why'd you choose it?"

"I wanted to see how long you'd wear something for me." The corners of her lips curved as she tilted her head, waiting for me to say something. But I didn't know how to react. Val and Zena must have caught that because they made some excuse to get a milkshake somewhere before leaving. Now it was only me and Camille at the table.

I was about to open my mouth when she broke the silence. "I like you, Veo." Her eyes studied me, scanning me up and down then back up again. "You're sweet. Nothing like Noah, you know? I think I need that in my life."

I chuckled a bit, nervously before clearing my throat. She reached for my hand across the table. "It's soon, but. . . would you be my boyfriend for the next 24 hours?"

"For twenty-four hours?"

"Think of it as a trial period," she said slowly. "We try each other out."

With my fingers stuck in her hands as much as my mind was on her lips, I froze.

"So what do you say?"

I nodded. She held my hands in both of hers before Val and Zena returned. Val was talking on the phone nearby when Zena came over.

"There's going to be a little get-together at Val's place. You guys up for it?"

I drove Camille's car to drop Val and Zena at Val's place to prep. I, however, needed an actual change of clothes because I wasn't going to wear that embarrassing shirt any longer. I figured that Dad wouldn't be home soon. But once we pulled up to the rocky road leading to my house, I saw his pick-up sitting near the garage.

Whatever. I only needed clothes.

"I'll be right back," I told Camille before stepping out of the car. Inside, I found Dad on the phone, hanging up once he saw me. He had a stern look on his face as I entered.

"Where were you, Veo?"

"What do you mean? I was in school."

"Why are you wearing that then? That's not yours."

"A friend gave it to me," I lied before trying to get to my bedroom.

"Veo, come out here!" Dad called out. "Come out here now!"

When I returned, he was standing in the middle of the kitchen. "Miss Silvia actually asked me to come in today after school to discuss some things with you. But you weren't there. Where were you?"

Crap. I didn't know what to say. I could have lied some more, but I stayed silent.

"Where were you, Veo?"

Again, I stayed silent.

"Fine. You're grounded," he said. My mouth hung open for a bit, stunned, because he had never grounded me before. He never held that power ever since I was a kid.

"Go to your room, Veo," he commanded. But I shook my head and headed for the bedroom. I wasn't planning on staying. I grabbed whatever shirt I thought was mine and headed out. But Dad put himself between me and the front door.

"Where do you think you're going?" he asked.

"I'm going to a party."

"You're grounded, son. Go—"

"The hell I am." My heart raced. The wind blew, hitting the screen door that I was to pass. I couldn't tell what was about to go down with us. It felt like he was about to punch me, but I waited.

"Why are you like this?" he asked. It was a question that would make any kid feel like a fuck-up, stunning me into a corner that I refused to be stuck in.

"Why are you only being a father to me now?" I retorted.

After a moment, I knew that there would be no answers, so I passed him and returned to my girlfriend for the day.

THE PARTY WASN'T a big one, and it wasn't loud and lively. The living room was dark, lit by a little black ball equivalent to that of a disco ball. A table stood in the middle of the room holding a bunch of red plastic cups. There were only a few trays of food that were enough to feed the 20-25 people who came over.

By 10:00 p.m., I was filled with alcohol, and I was liking it. I had lost caring about who was there who would care about my behavior or my strange shirt that I still hadn't changed. And I'd gotten to the comfortable level with Camille. I remember planting a kiss on her and hugging her before she told me she had to use the toilet. Of course, I didn't follow, so I talked to Val, who sat on the other end of the couch.

"Val, are you, um, okay?" I asked.

"Yeah, I'm good. You having fun, Veo?"

"I am. This is a, uh, an, uh, fun night. We should do this more often."

She looked down, and even in my drunk state, I could see that she was sad. Maybe she was a sad drunk. "What's wrong?" I asked.

"Nothing," she said, staring at me. After a few moments, I believe that she deemed me as someone who wouldn't remember this conversation, so she continued. "I just hate my dad. I don't like my mom. She's sleeping around. They're like people who forgot that they had kids, I guess."

"You're not alone on that," I chuckled. "My dad does meth, man. My dad doesn't care. Fuck him! Don't let it get to you."

"Uncle Dan does ice?" she asked. I nodded as she stared off at a wall. "Our parents are useless."

"Mmm. . . not my mom though," I said before accepting another round from Val.

"I wonder if they'd feel anything if I fucked you," Val said.

"I don't know. But I think you're pretty. You're very, very pretty actually. Just like my girlfriend over there."

She smiled. "Oh, you are very tempting, Veo." That was the last thing I remember hearing.

YOU DON'T EVER hear much about a drunk guy getting raped, because it doesn't take a lot to get their blood flowing into the right places. I wasn't about to dive into the subject, but the question was popping up as I stood by her bed in my underwear, staring at her.

It was the morning after. I woke up with a headache being the first to greet me, then the air conditioner that buzzed as loud as an airplane, then the sight of Val sleeping right next to me in a thong. Once I saw her, my body jolted me out of the bed.

What the hell.

I tried to recount the events of last night, but so much blurred in my head with the headache. You would think that if you got laid the night you decided to let loose with your new hot girlfriend, it'd be with her. But Camille was nowhere in sight. It was only me and Val in the room.

A pang of guilt swept through my chest as my brain tried to sink in the reality that I had lost my virginity to my cousin. I threw my head back, rubbing my face, trying to make sense of it all. *Okay, Veo. This is okay. Cousins have sex. It's okay as long as they don't get pregnant.* But fear struck me hard at the thought of raising a kid this young in my life. I felt for anything plastic underneath my underwear but found none. The bed was clear of condoms too. Nothing on the floor. And there were no wrappers nearby either.

Shit.

Taking deep breaths, I stared again. My body was heating fast, wanting to punch the wall, but I left instead.

I put my clothes on beforehand. But once I opened the door, I found several people sleeping on the couches and floor of the living room. One of them was Camille who had her legs tangled with some guy. My guilt was released. I could have been angry. I should have been angry, but I was more confused.

I made my way through the living room until I saw someone up—John, Val's brother. He looked like he had woken up, but he held a pipe in his hand with a lighter in his other. I must have been staring, because when he noticed, he said, "Only got enough for one, man. Sorry."

I nodded, breaking out of my stare, and headed out the door.

AFTER COMING HOME to Matthew telling me that Seung and Ding had been calling non-stop about the barbecue pit, I called them back. They gave me their cell phone numbers after telling me more details and hanging up.

Although everything in my body was telling me to skip out on it, a beach day sounded like what I needed.

"After lunch, we're going to work on the yard," Dad said once he came out of his room.

"Uh, can we do that tomorrow, Dad?" It was a useless question. Even a weird question to ask when I'd made a disrespectful outburst the day before. But I didn't want to repeat yesterday in any way. The yard was something he would never disregard if he thought it had reached a point of unkempt. Heck, even I would agree that the yard needed work.

"Dude, just stay. You haven't been helping around the house," Matthew said. I rubbed my face, frustrated. Today wasn't going so smoothly. Saying nothing more, I plopped down on the loveseat couch. I watched Matthew play his choice of video game before scanning both of my brothers over, remembering John. I guess that I could have it worse. I could have it much, much worse.

The corners of my mouth curved. It'd still be a good day to be a family day, so I called Seung up to apologize. I told him to cancel my part in the barbecue because my dad wanted the yard cut and cleaned today.

"Oh, we'll help you! We'll be there soon!" he said, ignoring what I was saying. Before I could say anything, he hung up.

"Okay. Your call for your birthday," I muttered as if he were still on the line.

Dad called me to eat at the table. Corned beef and rice for lunch. I hadn't eaten since the night before, so my entire meal was gone in two minutes. After washing my dishes, I headed outside to set the bush-cutter up. But once I opened the screen door, I saw Ding's car pull up in the yard.

I shook my head, feeling a laugh come on at the thought of them doing yard work. *These guys*, I thought. *They never listen.*

Ding came out and took the bags of meat out of the

trunk. "Veo!" he yelled out, excited. Seung joined him after grabbing the case of sodas.

"I told you guys to cancel."

"Nonsense, Veo. We'll help you out! It'll be three times faster if you have three guys working on it, right?"

"Matthew and Dominic are helping too, so—"

"Even better!" Ding interrupted. I heard the front screen door slam behind me, and out came my dad. "Mr. Mafnas! We're here to help," Ding said, sounding like a little kid show character.

"Oh. Even better," he said, repeating after Ding.

"Afterwards, can we use your grill to barbecue?"

"Of course. But after the yard."

Dad went inside while Ding and Seung went on about how they knew that my dad would help them if they didn't know how to do something. But what followed was a rude awakening for them.

My dad wasn't the most lenient when it came to yard work. It needed to be done a certain way, and trash needed to be put away at a certain time. They didn't know that until they thought they were finished cutting the grass. My dad came out to ask them, "You guys taking a break bush-cutting?"

Ding was taken aback, but he answered stammering, "No, uh. We're actually finished."

"That's not finished, boys. Go back and finish."

I would have laughed, but I did feel bad for them, because their smiles dropped. Ding looked back at the grass, wondering what else could have been done. There were ditches in the areas that he touched because he held the bush-cutter too close to the ground.

"You're also kind of leaving a big area around the flower bushes over there," I tried to tell him.

"If I cut any more, it's going to cut that bush itself."

"Alright, alright," I held my palms up in surrender. He went back to working on the grass, but eventually, I took the bush-cutter from him and did it myself.

Seung, on the other hand, took on the dog poop and leaves on the ground that needed to be raked up and thrown away. He wasn't the most physically active person, so he took plenty of breaks. Each time he did though, his breaks wouldn't last very long, because Dad would come out and ask him about the progress of the yard. Although I'm sure that my dad wasn't frustrated, Seung admitted to me later on that he thought he was. Dad's frustrated face was enough to scare Seung off the property and forget about the barbecue altogether.

That time, I couldn't hold back my laugh.

THE SMELL OF freshly cut grass hung in the air and finally, the yard work was complete. Dominic was already in the shower when I sat on the steps with Ding and Seung plopping down on the chairs in the garage, exhausted. They didn't look like they wanted to do anything more.

I glanced at the clock inside the house. "It's 4:45. You guys still want to barbecue?" All I heard was light groaning from the two.

The screen door opened behind me and in an instant,

Ding and Seung straightened their backs. "You guys going to barbecue?" my dad asked.

Ding and Seung only stammered with their words. I could only guess that they were searching for some excuse, and I was right about that. "No, Mr. Mafnas. We didn't even marinate the ribs," said Ding.

"I actually marinated the meat for you guys two hours ago."

"Oh," Seung started, "well, we don't even know if the others are coming."

I threw him a look and took his phone, searching for the messages from the others. "You just got a text from Jason that they'll be here at 6."

Ding only scratched his head. After a few seconds of awkwardness from the two, Ding gave in. My dad went inside to check on the ribs.

"I told you guys to cancel the barbecue before," I sang.

"I didn't know your dad was that hard on that type of stuff," said Seung.

"Okay, well, who wants to barbecue the meat?" I asked. Seung looked away, pretending that he didn't hear my question. "Because I'm not going to do it," I said. Seung stood up and walked off somewhere.

Ding picked up his head and shook off some imaginary stress. Taking a deep breath, he did his superhero pose with his fists on his waist and his chest puffed up. "I'll do it. I'm sure your dad will teach me well."

"Did he teach you well with the yard?"

He didn't answer. I don't think he wanted to listen, so I held my hands up in surrender yet again.

What followed was Ding going inside to handle

the meat. Seung returned for drinks in the garage. And Dominic joined us later. Jason and the others made it later as well. At that point, my dad was hovering over Ding's shoulder, watching how he cooked the meat.

Seung must have been expecting some remark because he looked like he was holding his breath. But my dad finally opened his mouth. "You flipped it just in time. If you flip it and the meat stays on the grates, it wasn't ready to be flipped. But you flipped it at the right time. Good job."

Seung relaxed a bit. But I knew how my dad was when it came to cooking. Much different than when it came to the yard. That's why I was relaxed in the chair. Soon the jokes and the stories started. I guess my dad thought that music was missing, so he put his stereo by the screen door and played his songs. Out came a familiar tune that played often in movies. The guitar strumming was recognizable in two seconds.

She sang a song not long ago
Always at night, even in a storm
So don't worry, there's still light in the dark

While we're here, and after our time
They'll hear her voice, and they'll hear mine
So don't worry, my dear, you're in a good story

All was at peace at my place. That day, that emotion, love, never left the house. I was right where I needed to be.

That day was also the day that Matthew picked his new girlfriend up from her place to meet us all. Her name was Kayla.

TRACK #12
She's a Whole Other World

When I was 16 years old. . .

I WAS SITTING by the corner of the living room, using the computer when this song played on my dad's stereo system. The beat that might as well have belonged to a 50s movie soundtrack bounced around the room, livening up the night air from outside. I heard the loud rumbling of a car in the yard, and I figured that it must be Matthew finally coming home after leaving before 5:00 a.m. to be with Kayla. I was right.

Once the words of the song came on, the front screen door slammed behind Matthew whose mouth started syncing to the words of the song. What followed was a sequence of movements from him that I never thought I'd see. It was as if he had been secretly taking theater classes, and finally felt comfortable breaking out of that shell.

It was the most love-struck that I've ever seen my brother.

She's a whole other world
How she lives, how she breathes
She don't need a whole lot to be happy
In that, I got everything I could ever want

Oooh

She treats me just right
Even with a smile, she's enough
Oh, my girl, she's a whole other world
How'd I get this whole other world?

As his arms flew gracefully in the air and his head bobbed to the catchy rhythm of the song, jokes assembled themselves in my head. But even if I said them out loud, I was sure that they wouldn't strike Matthew with a hint of embarrassment if he were already dancing like this in front of us. For the last two months, I had never seen him happier. Of course, he'd be smiling when she was around, but even when she wasn't, he was searching for her. At one of his football games, I saw him making his way to his team on the field. But he was scanning the crowd for something or someone, and I'm pretty sure it was her.

The girl even made her mark in our refrigerator. The only tasty bottled drinks in there had her name on it with Matthew's handwriting, which always killed my excitement when I thought it was something open to the whole house.

As the song ended, I forgot all the insults I was preparing to pierce him with as he plopped down on the couch, asking what Dominic was watching on TV. I shrugged it off, figuring that if I forgot it, it probably wasn't as good to mention. But once I turned my attention back to the computer, I noticed the pink plumerias that Matthew laid out on the coffee table.

Probably some weird couple thing he was having with Kayla.

I HADN'T FORMED much of an opinion on Kayla until the day after Matthew's musical number. The times that I did see her before then, she was quiet. Her hair was long and ridiculously straight (something girls called "rebonded"). Her face was clean and attractive all because of the mole that sat by her lip that Matthew considered a sexy mark. A smile could have sent her to model agencies or beauty pageants, placing her in the top spots, but she didn't smile much. She had her face buried in her phone each time I saw her, except for the first night I met her. She didn't pull out her phone at all then. I believe that was the first and only time I saw her smile, and that was only to greet everyone. But afterward, she sat and disappeared off to the dark corner of the garage with Matthew, who was intrigued with everything she whispered about that night.

I was lying awake on the couch the morning after Matthew's performance. It was 6:00 a.m. Dominic, Dad, and I were in the living room. Dominic crashed out on the futon with my dad asleep on the other couch when I heard the front screen door creak behind the closed wooden front door. Keys dangled and hit each other from the other side of the door, accompanied with Matthew's voice telling Kayla to stay quiet because we were all asleep inside.

"Got it," Kayla said. Once they managed to unlock the door and come in with what sounded like plastic grocery bags, I shut my eyes, not wanting anyone to know I was awake yet. I wasn't ready to talk to anyone and still wanted my thoughts to myself. But that was killed off by my curiosity of what Matthew and Kayla were talking about once they got to the bedroom. It started off with Kayla asking if Matthew got the oyster sauce she asked him to get when they were in the store. That grew to questions and remarks that would have unsettled anyone.

"Why weren't you listening? Too busy texting Sarah?" I heard her say. Matthew was arguing back, saying that he didn't even talk to her, and that he put his phone away whenever they were together.

"Yeah, so why didn't you get the oyster sauce, Matthew? You even left the aisle for it. Where did you go?" Matthew tried to recall what he did, then said that he remembered that he was texting Asher, and he must have forgotten when they stopped.

"You put your phone away, my ass," she mocked.

There was a pause in their conversation. I imagined Matthew standing there, nodding his head off, taking the verbal abuse from her. But what came next was a first. I'd never heard him ever say that to a girl.

"Holy crap. What? Are you on your period today?"

The argument then went on for a while, dipping into every other topic that seemed to have bothered either one of them, like how the air conditioners in our place were never on and how Kayla only drove to see him once a month and how sloppy our bedroom was when she came over and how much she complained about whatever he did in school. They went on and on, getting louder and louder, eventually waking everyone else up in the house. Once Dad stood up and walked to the bathroom, their argument ceased. Matthew knew from the sounds of footsteps on the hollow floor that someone else was awake. I couldn't tell if they were arguing in whispers, because I heard nothing else from them for a while. But I opened my eyes when I finally heard them entering the kitchen, sorting bags of groceries, pretending like their argument didn't happen.

Kayla didn't meet anyone else's eyes, probably still pissed. I knew she was hoping nobody had heard them. But Matthew leaned on the couch with a smile, a very convincing one too. "Morning! Kayla is cooking for us today!"

About a month had passed, and the arguments continued. I could tell that Kayla wasn't stupid, but she seemed to start thinking that the walls were a lot thicker than they looked. The beginning of an argument would quickly escalate to the point where everyone, in and out, would be aware of a couple fighting in the house.

Of course, they had good times, but that only was according to Matthew. Personally, I never saw them.

I was using the computer, searching for any info on *Tekken 5* characters. At the time, that type of info was limited, so I was having a hard time finding what I needed. The front screen door slammed shut with Dad coming in holding a handful of fishing gear. He wore his shorts, his vest over a light shirt, and his hat to protect his bald head. By the look on his face, I could tell that he caught something. Otherwise he would have been filled with frustration with all the stuff he was bringing in.

"Hi, Dad," I replied in a low voice when he greeted me, keeping my eyes locked on the screen.

I felt Dad's heavy hands on the back of my chair. His curiosity was piqued but fled fast. Seeing that video games were not something that his attention would latch onto for more than a minute, it didn't surprise me that he turned the faucet on to wash the dishes before starting on his catch of the day.

"How's your day, son?" he asked me, like he seemed to always do now. But I didn't pay much attention to it.

"It's okay," I said. Right then, I heard Kayla and Matthew emerging from the bedroom. Matthew was asking if she had all the things she needed, but Kayla only sounded irritated. It took only one glance to understand why. Her hair was a mess with her face looking like she had spent the day in a desert. She wasn't used to this house even though she had been dating Matthew for a while. Although the typical person would pity her, I couldn't hide my laughter well as I swung to face the wall. The girl looked like a pretty, high-maintenance daughter of a rich man who had recently learned the ways of living with the working-class.

Once she was out the door, I heard the car engine start right away. I already knew it was because she wanted the air-con on, but before a sound could come out of my mouth, I felt Matthew's hand hitting the back of my head. "Stop it," he said before turning to the man with the fish.

"Hey Dad, can Kayla sleep over?"

Dad glanced at him before continuing with the fish. "She just left."

"Yeah, she needs to cool down, so can she sleep over?"

"I don't know, son. Can she?" Dad raised a brow. "She knows we don't have air-con here."

I swung the chair back to face the screen as I bit my finger to hide my laugh, listening.

"She can handle it." The lie in Matthew's voice was obvious. I could only imagine what his face was like at that moment. But if I turned to watch, I knew the conversation would only end there.

"Alright. If you think she can handle it, then it's up to you."

Matthew thanked him and started for the bedroom, but he stopped in his path, returning to Dad. "She challenges me. And challenges, they make a man. . . she makes me stronger. I'm sure you've had a woman that was as strong as Kayla who kept giving you problems to solve."

Dad answered with no intent to disagree with Matthew, but Matthew kept on. "And women as beautiful as she is are supposed to have flaws, otherwise they aren't people. She and I are going to work through all this. It's still early for us, you know?"

I think Dad knew that Matthew had to fight his own battles to learn the lessons he needed to learn. But as Matthew kept on with the struggle to convince him that she was a good girlfriend, the pans started banging louder, the cuts and chops on the cutting board sounded when they didn't need to at all, and the fish was slapping a lot harder than it needed to. Dad was growing frustrated. The sounds of the items being thrown into the sink was getting louder and he was cursing under his breath as he scaled the fish.

"She keeps me from being bored! And I like that because I'm always on my toes when she's—"

"*Lańa' dai.* Son, you know the ring on the caribou's nose?"

"Yeah? What does that have anything to do—"

"You have that on yours, Matthew! She's pulling you around like an animal!"

Matthew tried to fight it, continuing with the arguments that painted Kayla in a good light. But it didn't last long.

"You're fucked up, son! That girl! She's got you fucked up! And she's making a liar out of you because I know you don't believe all that junk you just said!"

Matthew nervously laughed as Dad picked up the knife and turned back to the fish. The air grew awkward fast.

"*Ai*, son. There are lessons to learn in life, and if Kayla is one of them, then I'll welcome it."

Matthew didn't know what to say, so he only asked again, "So can she sleepover?"

Dad shook his head, trying to calm down. "Yeah, go for it."

"Thanks," he said before heading out the door. I could hear his voice pick up, probably telling Kayla that she could sleep over for the night. But his voice escalated, matching Dad's tone just a second ago. I made my way to the screen door to eavesdrop.

"Fine then! Stay at your place! But I'm not coming over even if you say you miss me," he said before hanging up. He grunted then silently threw a fit so Dad wouldn't hear. I hid for a bit, not wanting him to stop for my sake. When I returned to the door, I found him sitting on the front steps.

"Matthew," I called.

He looked back at me. "What's up?"

"What time is Kayla coming back?"

"Uh, well, something came up. I'm gonna head to her place tomorrow instead."

I nodded before opening the screen door. I took a seat in the plastic chairs in front of him, deciding to be an older brother.

"Matthew, Kayla seems like a pretty girl, but do you think she's right? I mean, for you?"

"What do you mean? Of course, I do. What the hell. What kind of a question is that?"

"It's just so early and it doesn't seem like it's even working."

"You're not always there, Veo. You don't have a lot of experience to tell me how a relationship works either."

"Yeah, you're right," I chuckled, trying to ease the conversation. "I know it's not my place to say anything, but she's just not giving me good—"

"And you're right. It really isn't your place to say anything." He stood up, about to go back inside before he continued. "By the way, Val is pregnant. You're a dick if you don't check up on her."

SARAH. KAYLA ALWAYS dropped that name when she was pulling another girl into the argument with Matthew. I never really wondered why, because I knew she was only jealous even if Matthew didn't do anything with her. But I soon found out why.

When school started up again, it was the beginning of my junior year. Both of my brothers were now in the same school as I was. By this time, Matthew had already hit his growth spurt, and within a couple of weeks, our group of friends was already determined. Funny thing was that whenever someone found out that we were brothers, they'd be surprised. "You guys don't even look like you're related," I'd hear a lot. It seemed like we had different interests and personalities, but we always got along. And even if we didn't, I'd still look out for them. So when I heard Matthew's name in a nearby conversation during lunch, I listened in. It was coming out of a girl's mouth that I didn't recognize. When I turned for a look, I figured that she must have been in my brother's class.

"Matthew's cute," she giggled.

"Well, you're lucky. He kept flirting with you in class today," said another girl.

"Oh, stop it, Sarah. He wasn't. He's still seeing Kayla." The girl fake vomited as she dropped her name.

"Maybe he's going to break up with her," said Sarah.

"So?"

"Soo. . ." Sarah sang before she continued. "You just need to give him something to assure you like him too."

The bell rang at that moment. I couldn't hear the rest of the conversation with all the commotion going on. My interest in my brother's life disappeared as the rest of my uninteresting day went on. Though I did almost blow up something in chemistry class, resulting in Mr. Turner raging at me for one second. The next moment, he was explaining in a totally rational and professional manner why we should never mix certain chemicals together. He was one of those teachers that believed that the best way to learn a lesson is through making mistakes. After class, he asked me to stay back only to tell me to pursue some kind of science when I went to college. Maybe I should have told him that college might not be an option for me, but I'll always remember his answer when I asked him why. "Because your curiosity will take you far, Mr. Veo. Of course, you have to be more careful. But being as curious as you are, the world could benefit from a person like you in the sciences."

I nodded, disbelieving at first. But the words were sinking in, and I thanked him. For the rest of the day, I was left in my thoughts about what he had said. I was actually considering college now, which wasn't really something I thought much of since I knew of its expenses. I thought about it as the bell rang, on the bus ride home, and on the car ride my dad took Dominic and me to attend a rosary. I thought about it while praying, while eating, and on the car ride back home at night. But it disappeared in an instant, replaced with surprise once I heard moans coming from our bedroom. Dominic tried to open the front door only to find it locked. Dad banged loudly on the bedroom window. "Matthew! Stop what you're doing and open the front door! Now, Matthew!"

Matthew and another girl he introduced as Brianna rushed out.

"Hi, guys!" She nervously laughed with the voice I recognized from earlier that day.

IT DIDN'T TAKE long for Kayla to find out about Brianna, especially since the girls didn't like each other. Apparently, it hadn't hit Matthew that getting with Brianna was perfect material against Kayla.

After school on Friday, Kayla cried, arguing with Matthew who kept denying what happened.

"Then how did she know you have a birthmark on your ass, Matthew? Huh?! How did she fucking know?!"

"She could have seen that from PE!"

"You're such a fucking liar! Why did you cheat on me?!"

The arguments went on for hours until my dad went out. "Stop it, you guys. I'll drop you home, Kayla."

I didn't see what happened. I could only hear from inside. But I think Kayla only kept quiet since he stepped in. Matthew, however, stayed outside long after they left.

TRACK #13
Farewell

When I was 21 years old. . .

THIS SONG IMPRINTED in my mind.

Dad was asleep. He was like a cat now, a cat that stayed asleep unless some bodily function had to be met. And in Dad's case, that was either hunger or pain. His moments of wakefulness now altered the way he talked. It was difficult to have a conversation with him when he groaned with every answer. It wasn't the groaning that annoyed me. It was seeing how much pain he was in—whenever he was awake, he'd groan, his face would twist, and he'd hold his arm to his stomach. It was so strange how quickly it happened. Just last month, he was okay—he was doing everything okay and speaking okay. But it all changed so fast.

"Oy! Kayla! Dominic! Naomi! We gotta go now or we'll miss the flight!" Matthew yelled, blocking my view of the TV. I was sitting on the couch, pushing his legs away from my view, when he laughed. Sticking his butt out, he moaned like a girl—the usual joke he liked to make since I got back. He did it to every one of his friends. But he forgot that I knew him better than his buddies did. I knew how to counter him.

I locked him in an embrace that mimicked Kayla's. "Oh, my goodness! Let me have that delicious candy skin!" His face twisted. I could tell he was pulling as hard as he could to get out of my embrace. I made it worse.

"Cuddle me, big boy!" I moaned as high as my voice could get.

He yelled, finally breaking out of my hold. Coincidentally, Dominic, Naomi, and Kayla came out right then.

"Let's go, Matthew," Kayla said with a straight face. "My luggage is still in your room." Dominic had one arm around Naomi and the other holding luggage as they started out the door.

I watched Matthew lug Kayla's luggage, and I joined them once they were all outside. When all the things were in the trunk, Matthew came up to me. I held my arms out for a hug, backing him up.

"*Laña*," he cursed. But after clicking his tongue with a shaking head, I could tell he was grateful that I was staying behind. Someone had to take care of Dad.

"Are you going to be okay?" he asked.

"I'll be fine. We'll be just fine," I said, trying to pull up a genuine smile.

"I can stay if you—"

"No. Don't worry about us. Go see Mom. You told Dad you're leaving already, yeah?"

Dominic answered, "He's asleep. Couldn't tell him. We'll be back in a week though, so it won't be too long." I nodded as he continued, "You want to come drop us?

Naomi is joining us in a couple of days, so she's only driving us to the airport. She said she could bring you back here after."

"No use in it," I said as I pulled them in for a hug. "I'll see you guys in a week. Take care, brothers."

I watched as they headed for the car. Waving at them, I felt something weird that I hadn't felt in months, not since Hannah. I was in my home on Guam, the place where I grew up and met so many people. I could have gone to my Auntie Connie's place next door to avoid this feeling, but it would still be there. Loneliness.

I shook those thoughts away. It was just one of those days where my hormones kicked into gear. It would probably change the next day or maybe even in a couple of hours, so I headed back inside, trying to think of anything else.

Once I closed the screen door behind me, I heard Dad calling my name out. His bedroom was decorated with tons of medications. There were wrinkled but clean bedsheets sitting in each corner of the room, and cold air blew from the air-con that we installed for his comfort—anything to help ease his pain.

"Come on. Sit up," I said, putting my hands under Dad's pits, helping him get up. "You want soup? We have soup. Matthew made it."

Dad only groaned, holding his hand up onto his head, trying to rub the headache away. "Yeah," he said in a low voice.

I heated it up and then spoon-fed him. "Matthew and Dominic left not too long ago," I told him.

"Good."

I nodded, as he continued to groan each time he moved. He stopped taking the soup when I held it to his mouth and shook his head.

"Take some more, Dad. That wasn't a lot." He shook his head again. "Come on." But again, he only shook his head.

"Later," he said.

I pulled the bowl and spoon away and nodded, helping him lie back down. Once I saw he was a little more comfortable, I watched. His eyes were shut. His chest was expanding and contracting, lifting and dropping each time he inhaled and exhaled. His face was relaxing from being twisted the whole time he was awake. My dad was falling back into the only state that made him feel no pain.

I got up and collected the dishes. Then I told him that I would give him his medicine in an hour, though he probably didn't hear me.

The rest of the day seemed normal, which was to be expected. I gave Dad his medicine and he fell back asleep. I played video games. It was my day off, so I relaxed. My brothers were usually the ones who made things a little more exciting. But they were gone to Saipan, so I wasn't expecting anything.

But once 8:00 p.m. hit, the phone rang.

"Veo?" It was Auntie Connie's voice. It was shaky, and I heard her sniffling on her end of the line.

"What's wrong? Are you okay?"

"I'm okay, Veo. Where's your dad?"

"He's asleep."

"Can you wake him up?"

"I don't think that's a good idea. He's in a lot of—"

"Please, Veo. I need to tell him something."

I brought the phone to the room and woke my dad up. "It's Auntie Connie."

He picked up the phone. "Yeah?" he groaned. "Dun?" There was a pause. "I see. . . okay. Bye."

He hung up the phone and handed it back to me, before laying back down in the same pose as when I entered.

"What is it, Dad?" I asked.

"Your Uncle Dun. . . doesn't have much time left," he said, before knocking out from the pain.

THE WEATHER ON Guam relies on its humidity. When it is hot, it's humid. When it is raining, it's extra humid. The last night of 2013 was probably the best weather of the year. It was breezy and humid. There were a few clouds in the sky. But those clouds wouldn't stop people from going out. We'd all be anticipating the night show once midnight hit, especially in Tumon.

Excitement hung in the air. I felt it from where I was, but it wasn't contagious. I knew that people were excited, people who I wouldn't see tonight or possibly ever. I couldn't feel excited, because it was just another day tomorrow with a different number to put at the end of a date. What was so different about it?

But I suppose that this year had changed me. I looked back at my dad's closed bedroom door, knowing that he was still fast asleep on his bed. Whenever I got sick, I enjoyed sleeping so I wouldn't have to think about my nose being plugged or my body feeling weak. But I couldn't fathom having to sleep all the time to avoid this feeling.

My eyes traced the lines of the walls, leading me to the fridge, then the kitchen table, then the couches. The room was full of things, but no people. It's funny how empty a full room made me feel.

I turned my gaze back to the waiting darkness that dressed itself with clouds. Where was I a year ago? I knew I was in Seattle, but how did I spend my New Years' then? It was all fuzzy until I remembered where I spent the night.

Hannah and I were at a party that she liked to call a social gathering. She was dressed up nice—a short, black dress, with her hair up. She was wearing heels, which I remembered because the party was actually outdoors. It was something she hadn't expected, and she grew angry over the course of the night. Something about the back of her new heels scratching the back of her feet.

We were sitting at a table, talking to her friends when Hannah asked Veronica where the bathroom was.

"Oh, it's back there by the trees."

She was surprised to find the bathroom was a port-a-potty, though I'm not sure why, considering that she was the overdressed one at this party. She whispered to me that she needed to use the restroom.

"Oh. Yeah. It's back there," I pointed to it. She smiled nervously at everyone else at the table. "Come," she said when her smile dropped in my direction. She stood up, and I followed her to the back.

She disappeared inside the restroom and said nothing.

"Did you need anything?" I asked.

Again, nothing. I exhaled, and looking around, found

a pathway. I followed it to a hidden area, devoid of lights. Where there are no lights at night, there are stars. I looked up, finding the night sky filled with just that. Stars.

I spent a good amount of time there, watching the sky. Hannah must have been searching for me when she found out that I wasn't at their table. But it didn't matter to me.

Fireworks went off overhead and I watched as the sky lit up with colors. It felt nice to be away from everyone else.

Today, on the last day of 2013, my alarm went off. It was 11:45 p.m. and time to give him medicine again.

I poured some water into a clean glass before entering his room, unsurprised at finding him sleeping on his side. I got out what he needed from his medication box, then sat by his bed.

"Dad," I whispered, shaking him. "Dad. Medicine time."

"Veo?"

"Yeah, it's me. You gotta take your medicine."

"What time is it?"

"It's 11:45 p.m."

"What day is it?"

"It's Tuesday," I answered. "It's New Years' Eve."

"Oh? Then we gotta go outside."

"No. No, Dad. You've got to stay inside."

He ignored me though and got up. I kept repeating that he needed energy before his appointment the next day.

He took slow steps but made it to the doorknob. I grabbed a blanket and placed it over him, holding his arm over my shoulders. "Okay, Dad," I said.

We got to the living room where he sat on the couch. He faced toward the window where I'd stood moments ago to look over the breezy view of Tumon. I got his medicine and water from his room and gave it to him.

As he took the medicine, he said, "One year can really change things."

I only nodded. I thought he was going to continue, but when I looked over, his eyes were already shut. I couldn't tell if he was sleeping again, but I didn't bother waking him up.

Soon, I could see a spark out the window. My eyes widened as I saw fireworks setting off into the night sky. The corner of my lips lifted, but I felt a tug at my chest, telling me to look back. Once my attention wandered behind me, I found Dad's eyes still shut. I tucked him tight like I did years before. There were words simmering in me that wanted to escape, but even I didn't know what they were. I didn't even know what to think, so I just stared at the night sky that was lighting up, celebrating a day.

AUNTIE CONNIE CAME over the next day, insisting that a visit to Uncle Dun was necessary.

"I don't think my dad could take a car ride to the—"

"This is for you, Veo. You're not going to see him for a while," she said, her eyes meeting mine. At that point, the idea of losing a family member was introduced to me. There was this uncomfortable hold on me. It felt like demons were embracing my back but squeezing the organs inside me. I wished I could be punched and injured, bleeding. It was anticipation for the pain that was to come, and I knew that I could do nothing about it.

I thanked her and took her car, heading for the hospital. I drove with the line repeating in my head: *Your uncle's dying. Your uncle's dying.*

But as I tried to take in all the present senses to steer my thoughts away for one moment from the misery filling my life, I smelled the car. Auntie Connie loved this strong orange scented air freshener that always gave me a headache when the windows were up. But from the looks of it, she hadn't replaced it for a while. It cost less than $5, but she had been covering a large portion of Dad's medical expenses ever since she found out that a huge chunk of our paychecks was going to bills. But she was still well-off even when she contributed. Auntie Connie knew how to handle her finances. I realized her senses right now were probably like mine—numbing themselves. Probably to protect her from the pain of losing both of her brothers.

I pulled into the parking lot and walked into the building. It didn't take long to find Uncle Dun's room, but I wasn't expecting to find Val, John, their mom, and Val's daughter in there.

"Veo," Val greeted me, surprised as the little one held her hand with tired eyes. She gently got her daughter up and said, "Riri, go amen your Uncle Veo." Riri walked over to me and bowed her head. It was the first time any kid had done this to me. And with Uncle Dun in the room, it didn't seem right not to pinch her nose, which felt and looked a lot like mine.

She shook her head, waking up, and looked at me with

wide eyes. I smiled at her, pushing a little giggle out of her mouth. "Go back to your mom," I mouthed and pointed.

Auntie Lynn asked if I wanted alone time with him.

"Yeah. Please."

They all left the room. Now, it was just me with a man in a coma. There was no way that I'd know if he'd hear me, but my hope was still there as I started.

"Hi, Uncle Dun. It's Big Man." A sad chuckle came out of me, stopping short. I didn't know what to say. I was feeling a lot. But I stopped before any words depicting those feelings came out.

I took a breath in and one out. But eventually, I decided that this whole situation shouldn't change the way I reacted to him. He was the only one who still treated me the same after that whole mess in juvie. And I couldn't be more grateful, so I said it.

"Thank you."

THE NEXT MORNING, I was on the phone when my dad called out for me from his bedroom. "Veo!"

I hung up and went into his room, and unexpectedly found him on the floor, struggling to get up. I picked him up, asking what he was trying to do as I tried to help him back onto the bed.

"We gotta go to the hospital," he said, groaning. "You gotta see Dun."

"Dad. . .Dad, it's okay. You have to rest. I already saw—"

"No, you're not going to see him for a long time." I realized that Auntie Connie didn't tell him that I went to the hospital yesterday.

I nodded. "Yeah, I know. It's okay, Dad. Just rest. I already went—"

"I'll see him soon, but you need to go, son. Go. Go. I'll be okay here."

"Calm down. Calm down," I repeated.

"No! You're not listening to me!"

"Okay. Okay. I'm sorry, Dad. I'll go to the hospital now, but you need to take your medicine."

"I'll take it myself. Just go!"

"No," I said as I reached for the box of medications on the table opposite of the bed. "Here, let me get it."

"Fine! But make sure you go, son!"

I spilled out two large pills and handed it to him with the glass of water that sat on his side table. "Go to sleep, Dad."

He was lying back down before I left the room. "Make sure you go."

"I will, Dad. Just rest."

I stood by the door, watching him calm down and eventually fall asleep. I wondered how Auntie Connie was taking the news at the hospital, how things had changed even though it was only one less person. I walked to the window, pulled a bit of the curtain open, and stared at the chairs that my dad and Uncle Dun would sit on, talking while having a beer. Sometimes, they'd be arguing. Sometimes, they'd be calm. Other times, they'd just sit in silence, watching the island. It was one of those habits or rituals people had that could easily be taken for granted.

I stared at the chairs, wishing it would happen one more time. But it wasn't going to happen again. Uncle Dun wasn't going to be around to do that anymore.

"May our times…intertwine again, brother," I heard my dad mutter in his sleep.

It will be a while from this farewell
When we'll see each other again
But cheer up, Darling, 'cause though your head is low
You haven't truly lost a friend

TRACK #14
Shoreline

When I was 16 years old...

I SAT BY the computer desk in the living room, working on an application the night before my 17th birthday. I was trying to get Val off my mind. She had been ignoring me and pushing me away ever since I found out about her pregnancy. Every time she saw me calling for her in the halls, she headed for the girl's restroom, and we all know I couldn't go in there. She was avoiding me, and I didn't know why. The whole situation was ticking me off. But not tonight. I didn't want it to ruin my night.

A couple of hours ago, Seung introduced the idea of moving to California with him and some of the guys after graduation. It was a nice idea. A good opportunity to make something of myself. But California? I heard the place was expensive. If there was a place for me to make something of myself, it'd be Seattle, the headquarters of growth. But now seemed too early to talk about it, especially with the possibility of my being a father. I shook the thoughts off, deciding to ponder on it some other time.

The silence that was only visited by croaks and buzzes from the creatures outside got boring, so I shuffled the songs of the playlist I had set up earlier that month. The first song to come up was one I'd put on repeat for the past couple of days.

The pattern, structure, and melody were played on a piano. It had the ability to soothe me in a second. Three notes waved back and forth like a shore eating up the sand and pulling away. The words sung with a melody that always led my thoughts to a spot on the beach at night, watching a full moon. Everything that came from the stars and moon above bounced off into the water as the shore pushed in and out.

> *Down the shore, you've left me to stare*
> *At you that I couldn't read from here*
> *You've said you wanted me around*
> *But your soul, your heart was never to be found*
> *You're casting your shadow onto my mind*
> *As the one to never be mine*
> *But as I stand on this shore again*
> *I'm wishing to sink even lower in the sand*

I suddenly heard a guitar being strummed from the couch, matching the chords of the song. Unsurprisingly, it was my dad. I listened as he stumbled on the chords, making mistakes as he tried to learn the song by ear, though it didn't take him long to accomplish. Then the song ended.

"Play that song again, boy," he said, and I did. As the song went on, I watched and listened to him play. I was surprised that he liked a song made within the past ten years enough to want to learn how to play it, but then I remembered this wasn't the first time he heard this song.

He continued strumming until he picked at the individual strings, bringing the thoughts of a shore back. Soon, my image of the beach had him sitting on the sand with me, saying nothing, singing nothing. It felt like peace.

But the song brought it to an end, signaling him to put the guitar away. I could have played the song one more time, but he probably wouldn't have tried to pick up the guitar again, so I didn't bother. It was a nice moment, but all nice moments have an end.

"What are you doing?" he asked, heading for the kitchen.

"Just working on that application."

"Application for what?"

"Some honors club thing."

I felt his gaze over my shoulder that was soon a nod to my essay on reasons why I was a good leader and all that nonsense. I always found those essays to be full of bullshit, and I could tell that my dad thought so too.

"*On top of my leadership among my soccer team, I contribute to my circle of friends as a great listener, since that's what I feel is missing a lot nowadays: listeners,*" he read, chuckling by the end.

"Yeah, yeah, yeah. . ." I expected him to joke about how egotistical I sounded.

"Just keep working on it, son," he said, sounding encouraging as he went back to the fridge, looking for something to drink or eat. I must have stared at him because his brows raised at me once he caught me.

"What? Do you need help talking about yourself?" he asked, which surprised me even more.

I shook my head, feeling the corners of my mouth curve.

"Do you remember what you wanted to be before? You wanted to be an astronaut," he took a beer can from the fridge. "Do you still want to be an astronaut?"

"Not worth trying."

"Why not?"

"Well, we're not exactly rich."

"Don't ever let that stop you, son," he said before he took a sip of his beer. "You've got one life. At the end of it, you'll only have yourself to take to the grave. Not me, or your brothers, or your future wife or husband. Just yourself, your stories, your memories. You. So make yourself as interesting as possible. Even if you think you can't be an astronaut or go to astronaut school, you might as well try. You can laugh at the end of your life at your attempt, but at least you won't have regrets."

I didn't know what to say. I didn't know how to take advice from him. There was a heaviness in my chest that I didn't want to feel. Not from him. "Dad, do you think I'm gay?" I changed the subject to anything else, fake laughing.

He clicked his tongue. "*Ai*, son, I give you advice and that's what you take away from it?"

I shrugged, facing back to my work. I didn't need to hear the answer.

"It doesn't matter, Veo. If you are or if you're straight, you should know that I love you."

The heaviness reappeared and dropped in my chest like an anchor on land, hearing those words from him. The air grew silent between us. I didn't know what to say to him, but I knew he felt that heaviness too as he said, "Just tell me when you get accepted into this honors club. If there's some initiation event, I'll be there."

I looked back at him. My eyes met his, searching for anything that told me that he meant what he said. "Yeah?" he said.

I nodded, feeling my smile. "Thanks, Dad."

He looked down at his beer can before walking to the couches. He sat down and turned the TV on, filling the silence of the room with the theme song of a family sitcom.

I faced my work again, hoping that I'd get accepted into the program now.

IT WAS MY seventeenth birthday. A Monday. I thought nothing special was going to happen, since, like the rest of society, I hated Mondays. I didn't think much of my birthday either.

It started off like any other day. I came out of the bedroom to find Dominic and Dad already sitting on the table, both sipping gas store's coffee while Dad read that day's newspaper. Dominic threw his hands up in the air, all smiles, wishing me a happy birthday.

"It's not my birthday," Matthew said sleepily from behind me, but once he registered the day's date, he glanced at me. "Oh. Right. Happy birthday."

"So how's your day starting?" Dad asked me as I took a seat.

"Starting off right, Dad." Everyone reached for some bagels and pancakes. As Matthew started waking up, his lips curved wider and wider until he announced some news.

"So, as you all know, I've been working on everyone's yard here, been taking some extra shifts just to make some more money—"

"And I always ask why you're trying to make more—" Dominic started.

"I'll be getting to that, young Dominic. Please, please. No interruptions," Matthew said elegantly before excusing himself to run back into the bedroom. He returned with his hands behind his back.

"So, as I was saying, I've been trying to get more money so I could get Kayla a proper ten-month anniversary gift."

I was already rolling my eyes. An anniversary is a year thing, not a month. And either way, I never understood monthsary gifts. But hey, to each, their own.

"And I got her this," Matthew opened a little box to show an expensive-looking ring with a pink sapphire gem. I raised a brow, seeing Dominic and Dad do the same.

"Wow, son. That looks. . . pretty," Dad said.

"Dude, how much was that?" Dominic asked.

"The price doesn't matter, bro. It's a gift for Kayla."

"Matthew, are you sure you want to give her something that pricey? It's not even your one-year anniversary yet," I asked.

"Yes. Yes, I do."

"You know that you guys have been kind of fighting—"

"Dude, Veo, fucking hell, yes, I know. That's why I want to fucking give it to her."

"Okay, okay, son. It's a beautiful ring. Go, give it to

her," Dad said, calming him down. "It's also your turn to get ready first. So, bathroom. Now. Get ready for school."

Matthew was still irate as he took his uniform into the bathroom. I was about to say something when Dad said, "It's his choice. Let him do what he wants."

Matthew heard that and came out, eyeing me. "Veo, you seem to be the only one with a problem with her here, so let me be clear. I'm going to laugh at you on our graduation day."

"Son, stop."

"I'm going to laugh at you on our first day of college together in the States, because I know she will come with me to whatever school offers me a good scholarship."

"Matthew. Matthew," Dad tried again.

"That's how much faith I have in our fucking relationship. And I'm going to laugh at you on our wedding day and when our first kid is born. So fuck off—"

"MATTHEW!" Dad yelled. "GO BACK IN THE SHOWER! Now!"

A second that felt too long passed before Matthew stomped back into the bathroom, leaving us to continue eating in an awkward silence.

Happy birthday to me.

THAT DAY, MY English class was the first class I had to learn something from. I remember that lesson even now. It was the hero quest: a journey a hero goes on that follows stages and trials, bringing them to a point of ultimate change.

I learned the stages that a hero goes through in a story. I learned about the call to adventure, the road of trials, and all that stuff. It was probably the only time in English class that I listened with interest. Then the bell rang.

"Okay, so that's all we'll be covering about the hero's journey, Class! Don't forget to work on chapters 19-20! And happy birthday to our Mr. Mafnas here!"

Everyone had ignored the first half of what Ms. Suzy was saying until she mentioned my birthday. Some were groaning, muttering insults my way as I now had the label as an incestuous teenage boy since everyone knew about Val's pregnancy. Others actually greeted me with an "Oh my god! It's your birthday? Happy birthday!"

But once it all stopped, I returned to my thoughts of the story I was going to tell. Mine. I stood up and finished putting all my stuff in my mesh bag. I puffed up my chest, took a deep breath, and narrated my thoughts to myself.

So what's your hero quest for the day going to be, Mr. Veo?

I headed out to the busy hallways and immediately saw Val. The fear I felt every time I saw her came back anew. The whole hero quest was now in the back of my mind. She didn't look like she was showing, and I admit that I was disgusted with myself every time I saw her. Not because she was gross or ugly, but because even when I'm drunk, I expect myself not to do anything with anyone I was related to. But life seemed to like fucking with me, testing my limits when I wasn't in control.

I was about to head her way when her eyes met mine. She quickly averted them and picked up her speed to avoid me at all costs. Sighing, I changed my mind and headed to my next class instead, brushing against many shoulders, arms, and bags. I wasn't paying much attention to whose it was until I brushed up against a familiar bony shoulder which was followed by a familiar voice from this morning.

"Sorry. Excuse me," Matthew said, not turning his head to see me. He kept walking with his friends, making me wonder where Kayla was. Since cheating on her, Matthew's arguments with her had been ongoing and stronger. Why she didn't break up with him, I didn't know.

I thought about the ring he was about to give her if he hadn't already. For a high schooler, whose source of income was the number of lawns he mowed, I could only assume that that ring was worth too much.

I watched his back as he walked to the end of the hall with his friends. He swung his mesh bag over his shoulders. Right then, I noticed his fat bag stuffed with his books, pens, bulky jacket, buttoned with a photo of his favorite baseball player, Barry Bonds, and the small box. The hallway was emptying, and I knew that the bell would soon ring, but at that moment, I knew my quest for the day. It was a small one, but it would be enough to spark something.

My goal by the end of lunch: save Matthew's ass from wasting his mowing of a thousand lawns, ninja-style.

PROJECT THOUSAND LAWNS was underway. Once the bell rang for lunch, I was outside, running through the crowd with my poorly packed bag. It was full of my books, jacket, notebooks, carving knife, and pens. Besides the carving knife that I could get anywhere, I didn't keep anything special in it. Everyone could see what was there, and I'd rather not have people consider taking whatever was valuable. So if anyone wanted to steal my bag, go ahead! There was nothing there!

I raced my way to the cafeteria to find Matthew's class already lining up (the benefits of being the class nearest to the cafeteria). As the cafeteria filled up with students, I stood by the door, wondering how to steal the Box of a Thousand Lawns. If I asked him to sort through his bag, he'd know that I'd gone through it once he found the box missing and blame me while still getting the box back in time to give to Kayla. So I knew that I had to get to his bag without anyone noticing.

I lined up to get my lunch once Seung came by, asking me if he could ask about Val. But the conversation didn't last long. I told him that I'd tell him what happened once she talked to me herself.

"Right. Right, but I'm super curious, and you're my friend, you know?" he continued on, trying to ask. His words were coming in one ear and going out the other as I continued looking for an opening. I was hoping that somehow Matthew would leave his bag somewhere without his friends around. But that would be a stupid thing to do. However, it wasn't long until exactly that happened.

Kayla arrived at the table with her lunch. Matthew left his bag with her, and in a couple minutes, she left the table full of bags alone.

I ran over, exposed on the empty side of the cafeteria, knowing I had to be quick. I sped up, looking through his bag for the small box until I found it underneath his bulky jacket that seemed to be holding something else.

"What are you doing?" Kayla asked behind me. I held the small box in my hand behind my back.

"Oh, uh, I'm just, uh. . ." Fuck. I've always been a terrible liar.

"Veo?" Matthew's voice sounded behind me as I straightened my back, tightening my fists into balls. "What the hell are you doing?"

I turned to see he was already pissed. He put his tray down on the table and yanked his bag behind me. He sorted through whatever his jacket was wrapped around in his belongings, finding everything in there, except for the small box. Then he grabbed my wrist, whispering loudly with his nose an inch from mine. "Outside. Now."

The Little Bitch Look was something I saw in a lot of Matthew's opponents whenever he got into fights (and he got into many fights). It always had a tiny hint of *Shit, I'm in trouble.* But I knew what I was getting myself into. I clenched my jaw with the small box still in my hand, refusing to give him the look.

We were heading for the corner of the campus where no faculty would find us. Our route was stopped short when Matthew pulled the box from my hand, pushing my back harder than he should have. I threw a punch at my own brother within sight of the principal's main office.

"Dude, what the fuck? Why'd you have to push me?" I held out my arms at him as he stumbled back.

"You little fucker!" he yelled as he right hooked me. Soon, we were in a ball of fight that attracted the attention of many students.

"You're such a disrespectful bitch, you know that?!" he yelled again when I fell back, but I tripped his legs and quickly had him in a hold that he broke out of. The match was broken up by Mr. Zinger and Mr. Brown after a couple minutes. As Mr. Brown held Matthew back, he screamed, "You know what?! AT LEAST, I DON'T FUCK MY COUSINS! Yeah, you sad piece of shit! You're not even talking to her, are you?! What kind of man are you?!"

"That's enough. THAT'S ENOUGH!" Mr. Brown commanded. Then we were towed to the principal's main office.

MATTHEW WAS CURSING under his breath when Val came in with her bag, taking the seat beside him. I sat up straight, looking at her, but she was avoiding my gaze.

"What are you doing here?" Matthew asked her, still irate.

"I got called in."

"Val?" I tried to get her attention. "Val?"

No answer.

"Val, come on. Talk to me. If I'm gonna be—"

Mr. Zinger shushed me as he came in with our bags, triggering Matthew to let go of his angry expression as he reached for his. But Mr. Zinger pulled it back. "You guys aren't getting these back yet."

"What do you need them for?" Matthew asked. But Mr. Zinger didn't answer. He had the feel of a cop, which ticked Matthew off as he slumped down in his seat. He looked both worried and frustrated, cursing again.

"Quiet," Mr. Zinger commanded.

Moments later, Dad, Uncle Dun, and Auntie Lynn came in.

"Dad?" Val sounded surprised.

"Thank you for coming in. I believe you guys were made aware of the fight between the two boys here," Mr. Zinger said as Mrs. Ocampo stepped into the light from her dark office. She shook our parents' hands before we all entered her office.

"Mrs. Ocampo, while I'm sure Duane here is concerned about his nephews, I'm not sure why Valerie needs to be a part of this visit," Auntie Lynn said once we sat down.

"Ms. Acosta, I'm sure by now that you know—and if you didn't, you must know now—that, well, Ms. Valerie, would you prefer to tell her yourself?"

Val took a deep breath, sat up in her seat, but slouched back down, saying nothing.

"Alright then. Your daughter here is pregnant."

My dad shook his head, muttering something before he spoke up. "Ms. Ocampo, just because Dun here is my brother does not mean that my sons and I should be here for this type of conversation."

My pulse quickened, realizing why I had to be here.

"Well, you and your eldest here need to be here. There has been word that it is your son who is the father, Mr. Mafnas."

All eyes, except for Val's, were on me, pushing the heat of my body to rise. I didn't know what to say.

"Is this true?" my dad asked me.

Val grunted and rubbed her face with frustration, coming clean. "No, it's not."

"It's not?" I asked.

"No, we didn't even do anything." She straightened her posture before she mumbled her next words. "That morning we woke up in my bed, I just took off our clothes and slept."

"Then why didn't you just tell me? You know I've been trying to talk to you, and you—"

"Shut up, Veo," Uncle Dun said in an intimidating tone that I never heard him use before. The room fell silent before Uncle Dun asked his daughter, "Why'd you do that, Valerie?"

She scoffed. Uncle Dun's breathing was growing louder and faster, trying to hold back from exploding. "Why did you do it, Valerie?" he asked again.

Again, she scoffed, shaking her head.

At that point, I could feel Auntie Lynn's temperature rising too. It was getting uncomfortable sitting next to her. The tension in the room was growing alarmingly fast. Mrs. Ocampo broke the silence, asking the three of us to leave the office for a little bit for her to sort things out with Val and her parents. But as we made our way out, Uncle Dun yelled his question, "Why'd you do it, Val—"

"Oh, shut your mouth, old man. I knew this would happen! You're only a 'good man' to everyone but your own family. You were never around. You're only here because of Veo!" The door closed behind me. Matthew, Dad, and I were back to standing in the main office again.

We weren't off the hook, but there was an enormous weight lifted off my shoulders. Dad wasn't looking straight at us yet though. He excused himself, asking Mr. Zinger where the restrooms were and went out the door in search of it, leaving me and Matthew alone.

My brother sat down, but I remained standing next to the door until I grew curious about why Matthew was hanging his head so low. The air around him grew heavy and melancholic. He had a mood that I wouldn't have expected from a guy who was in trouble for things that had sent him to the office before. I took the seat two chairs away from him. A couple of minutes passed before he opened his mouth.

"Why'd you have to touch my stuff? It's none of your business what I do with the ring anyway. You could have gotten in trouble."

I furrowed my brows. He wasn't making sense. "Why would I get in. . . never mind, Matthew. You're too stunned by this 'hot chick' to listen to any of us when we say that she isn't exactly good for you."

"Even if she isn't, that's for me to learn. I don't get why you gotta control my life, like how you tell others that my favorite food is tilapia when it's not or how you act like you're Dad when you're not or how you even told me that I was going to be an astronaut when we were kids. Veo, come on, man," he dropped his head.

Mr. Zinger stood up from the desk, opened our mesh bags, and searched through them. Matthew, at that point, was defeated. "And now, I've lost a good future. All because I'm holding what's hers for one day. It's not mine. It's not fuckin' mine," he said under his breath to himself.

Dad returned as Mr. Zinger pulled the bulky jacket from Matthew's bag. Out fell a brown paper bag that I didn't notice when I was sorting through his stuff an hour ago. I looked at Matthew, finding his head dropped so low as he listened to the rustling of the paper bag as Mr. Zinger looked inside.

"Whose is this?" Mr. Zinger asked. Matthew was about to raise his hand when I stood up. Whatever was in there wasn't worth his future.

"It's mine," I said, not looking back at Matthew who I suspected was shocked.

Mr. Zinger picked up the phone and dialed.

"What's in there?" my dad asked him, but it wasn't until Mr. Zinger hung up that he answered.

"Other than an expensive ring, your son here is in possession of cocaine."

Everybody grew silent, especially Dad. Not even Mrs. Ocampo calling us back into the office or Dad's talk with the police changed the vibe between Dad and me.

I sat in front of Mrs. Ocampo's desk once she and Matthew stepped out, leaving me and my dad alone in her office.

I didn't know what to say, but I felt like I had to say something, anything.

"Why did you have Matthew's ring in your bag?" he said, breaking the silence.

"I-I'm sorry, Dad," I managed.

But he didn't say anything. He only scratched the back of his head.

THE DAY FELT like it lasted a month. By the time we got to go back home, it was dark out. Dad hadn't said anything to me, and he went straight to his room once we arrived. I heard his door close, and the lights to his room shut off not long after. At that point, all I could hear was my own breathing as I stood by his door.

"Veo," Matthew called. "Can we talk outside?"

I followed his motions since I was feeling numb in every limb of my body. My head wasn't functioning well either. By the time we walked past the garage and almost to the jungle, Matthew turned to me, scratching his head. "Thank you."

I nodded, still numb.

"I should explain though."

"Yeah, you should."

He took a deep breath. "Ever since that whole thing with Brianna, Kayla has been kind of mad. She's been threatening me and even saying that she wants to kill herself. I don't actually think she would, but I'd rather not test her on that. For our monthsary, she bought this. I don't know why. She just did. She gave it to me this morning when I was gonna give her the ring, but everything went to shit," he rubbed the stress off his face before his eyes met mine. "It's not mine, brother."

At that point, I pulled up every bit of energy I had to say what I wanted him to know. "Matthew, don't ever fucking go down this road. I don't care if it's yours or not. Just don't do it."

"I know! I won't. But I'm telling you I wasn't planning on doing this."

"Good," I grabbed his wrist and looked him straight in the eye. "Because if you do, this family is going to break."

"Alright," he said, nodding. We stood still for a moment before I started for the house. But I felt his grab on my wrist before he pulled me in for a hug.

"Thank you," he said again.

We went back inside.

My senior year of high school was the year that I finally got accepted into the honors club. Long story short, the faculty that decided on new inductees felt my essay to be pure. And they gave me a chance at my dream to possibly be an astronaut, even if it was a tiny chance.

The induction ceremony came on a windy Friday. The grass outside the auditorium smelt of freshly cut grass, making me envious of the soccer team that I hadn't been a part of for a while. But I still stood out there, watching for the people coming in to support the inductees. It was only a couple of hours ago that I'd asked my dad to come tonight.

"Can you make it?" I asked, watching him change the red wire in the bush-cutter. But he only muttered something and nodded. At the time, I thought he said yes. But standing outside the entrance of the room fifteen minutes before the ceremony began, I was starting to believe that he didn't hear me at all.

A *lei* was placed over my shoulders, breaking my search

for one person as I realized that Dominic and Matthew were right behind me.

"Eyy!" A grin broke out on my face, matching both of theirs as they patted and congratulated me. Of course, they pointed out how useless the honors club could be, but they were there, nonetheless.

"What are you out here for?" Dominic asked.

"Oh, I'm just. . . you know, waiting for Dad. Do you know where he's at?"

They both shrugged and told me they didn't know. They'd just came from their baseball practice and film club that was held after school.

"Veo! Come on! We gotta line up! Who's going to be walking you down?" Ms. Suzy asked from the door as the other inductees began lining up with their moms or dads.

"Uh, uh," I stammered.

"We'll walk him!" Matthew said.

"It can't be other students, boys."

That triggered Matthew into working some charm on the sweet lady. "But our dad is going to be late, ma'am. There's no point in having him walk alone, you know?"

"*Aii*," she scratched the back of her head.

"Please!" both Matthew and Dominic pleaded.

"Alright, boys. Go to your spots. No messing around! I mean it!" She disappeared into the auditorium as they joined me once we got to my spot in the line.

"We're proud of you," Dominic joked, faking a tear.

"My boy's all grown up!" Matthew joined in.

"Ahh, shut up." We all laughed, but as it died down, Dad's absence rang in my head. I surveyed the area one more time, leaving my hopes with each step my brothers and I took before we entered the room. I took a deep breath and cocked my head back, looking at the spiderwebs on the corners of the hallway. I wondered if this was the corner of the world I should be at a year from now, if I should be at any corner on Guam.

"So what's the *bida*?" Matthew asked.

"Hmm?"

"What are you going to do after high school? Your graduation isn't too far away."

My eyes dropped to the floor. I didn't know what to do. I felt like I needed to stay, but I also felt like I needed to leave. I wasn't going to grow if I stayed in that house and if I stayed on this island. And I hated to admit it, but it all depended on Dad.

Fuck.

I shook my head, and finally decided to treat the situation like flipping a coin. If he arrives before I take a step in the building, I stay. If he doesn't, I move. I took a deep breath before I looked up to search the area. He wasn't there.

I took a few steps, searching for him again. But he wasn't there. It wasn't long until I stepped into the building. I searched for him one final time. He still wasn't there.

"You guys?" I said.

"Yeah?" Dominic answered.

"I'm moving."

"Where are you going?" Matthew asked with an eyebrow raised, smiling. I took a second to think about it, but I knew where I wanted to go.

"Seattle. I want to get out of here."

We took several more steps before Dominic opened

his mouth. "You'll do well in Seattle, brother," he said, grinning.

"Yeah. You'll be doing that city a favor by living there, bro." Matthew nodded. "And don't ever worry about us. I'll make sure we're all okay. Just like you always do."

TRACK #15
Goin' Crazy

When I was 22 years old. . .

I SENT MYSELF on a pizza run on my day off. Pizzas at Pure Pizza cooked fast and the drive there and back would take 20 to 30 minutes. On this day, I needed to escape the silence of the house, especially after what happened the day before.

We had two cars, Matthew's gray sedan and my dad's pick-up that was just one problem away from being pronounced dead as a vehicle. I asked Matthew if I could use his car. He agreed, until Kayla came out of the restroom and told Matthew, "Where are your car keys? I'm gonna go to the store."

"Sorry, bro," was all he could say. But as I sat in the driver's seat of my dad's old pick-up truck, my mind felt at ease. It felt right wearing jeans in a car with leather seats that would only burn my skin with the sun's heat cooking the seat's fabric. I knew how to deal with this pick-up truck. I knew I had to have the windows rolled down with "Goin' Crazy" playing on the stereo. I felt like I was traveling back in time to my childhood. I was six years old again. There were no problems around me. All I had to worry about was the first grade and doing my chores. My mom would hug me wherever I was, even through the phone. And my dad, he'd be healthy, still lifting cars with his magnificent strength and keeping the lawn in check before the sun set for the day. It'd be the time when I didn't know he messed around with drugs, so it'd be the time when I was still his son.

The dreaming ended as I pulled up to the parking lot. Being sure to take my time, I focused my thoughts on the present, pushing away all thoughts related to my family. I didn't want to know any more of what was going on in my house. My gaze lingered onto the floor as the saying, "Step on a crack and you'll break your mama's back," repeated itself in my head. It was a little game of mine that was always cut short by my reaching the destination.

I looked around once I joined the line, examining how fast it was moving. For five minutes, I deemed it unmovable, because of the old worker who was taking her time with the orders. I figured that someone must have called out, placing twice as many responsibilities on her, but since I didn't work there, I didn't know for sure. I didn't care enough to ask though, and I didn't mind the wait.

I felt around my pocket for my phone when I knocked against the person behind me. I knew I was being rude by apologizing without looking at the person, but I did it anyway.

"Veo?" It took a second for me to recognize that voice, but once I did, I turned around to confirm my theory.

It was Ollie, a female cashier at Kikki's Breakfast

House. She was also the only one with short hair and I always imagined her as a fairy. Something softened in me once I saw her. The corners of my mouth were twitching, itching to smile ridiculously. It was an odd feeling to have at this time in my life.

She had a lopsided grin, waiting for me say something. But that grin was enough to strike me silent.

"Well?" she started.

"Well. . . what?" I finally managed to say.

"Well, you hit me, so I'm owed an apology, Sir Veo."

"Oh," I started, regaining my composure. "I'm sorry. . . for bumping into you." She nodded with the same expectant look still on her face, making me wonder if I missed anything else. "And. . . it's good to see you?"

"Why, yes, I'll let you buy my pizza," she said. "And it's good to see you too."

I laughed as I lost attention to what was happening with the line. She poked my arm and pointed for me to move forward. As I did, I couldn't help myself, even though my nerves spiked. "You know what? I'll cover yours, but only if you eat with me."

Time stood still as I waited for her answer, my body as uncomfortable as possible. My heart was freezing, while my mind yelled at me to run away and to start racing like Sonic or Flash, pumping blood to my skin that would eventually turn the color of wine if there was a long delay in her answer. I did the only other thing I could do instead of wait. I talked.

Not giving her enough time to respond, I opened my mouth to talk about how long we'd been lining up for pizza. But before I branched out to the exciting story of the longest line I'd ever been in, she put her hand on my wrist. Her touch froze me, shutting me up.

"Maybe we can next week. I've got an essay to write for one of my classes."

"Ah. Too bad then." But we both said simultaneously, "No pizza for Ollie."

Squinting at me, her smile remained. "Jinx."

I had hit the front of the line. After I placed my order for a box that would take ten minutes to cook, I waited in line again for the cashier, leaving me with my thoughts that led back to work at Kikki's Breakfast House.

There was one day when I couldn't eat anything for my break, so I sat in the break room alone. My stomach was vocal about it, especially since the smell of food was inescapable. It got even worse when a bigger female co-cook of mine named Letty came in with a plate of freshly cooked spam and rice. I always thought it was an odd thing to order at a restaurant. But maybe she had eaten too much of the fancy food and wanted the basics of Chamorro food.

She greeted me before taking a seat at a different table. She kept to herself, but her food was still bothering me so much that my stomach was yelling out at her to feed me. I knew she looked at me from the corner of her eye. Trying to hide that she heard my stomach growl, she faced away. As for me, I only felt embarrassed that my stomach was doing this to me. But after a while, I shook those thoughts off. Holding my head up high, convincing my stomach that it won't be eating for a while, I laughed and announced, "I'm hungry, and I'm proud!"

At that instant, Ollie entered the room. "You hungry,

bro?" she laughed as she sat next to me. "Here, you can have some of my spaghetti."

She pushed her container of food at me. I declined several times before she grabbed a plate from the shelf and put some on it for me.

"Thank you," I said, finally accepting it, holding back the pride that I had a few minutes ago.

"No. Thank you. You're gonna eat that and tell me what you think." She told me that she had taken up cooking. She continued with her stories in the kitchen, but as I took a bite of her spaghetti, I felt every organ in my body contract. It tasted like she had dumped half of the black pepper container on it and mixed it around.

"So. . . how is it?" she asked with hopeful eyes. I could only cough and thank her for sharing her food with me, and that was enough to make her laugh. "I knew it was terrible. I put too much of something, right?"

"Yeahhh," I said. "Kinda."

"I put too much garlic in."

I probably didn't hide the surprise well, because she laughed again. "I'm just kidding. I know I put too much black pepper. I know. But hats off to you, Mafnas. I know how you hide the truth now. You're certainly not a liar."

After a few bites of her own cooking, I saw her face shift. I couldn't tell if she was getting sad about something else, or if she was getting insecure about her own cooking. But I opened my mouth.

"Hey. Ollie, have you tried Updog?"

"What's 'Updog'?"

"Nothing much. What's up with you?" I laughed. By

this time, I expected girls to roll their eyes like Letty did. But Ollie chuckled a bit before bursting out laughing.

"That's a good one, Veo. That's a good one."

I broke out of my flashback when the cashier called out to me. I paid and took a seat. As soon as I'd sat, they called my name to pick up my box. Ollie walked past me with her eyes on her phone. "Hey, Ollie. Can you wait a second?"

"Uh, sure," she said, looking at her phone. Once I got the pizza, I ran back to her. But as we started leaving, her eyes were still on her screen. I never pinned her as a person who thrived off social media, so I couldn't help but wonder. "What are you looking at?" I asked as we started for the doors.

"Paycheck. We got paid today. But this doesn't look right. I'm pretty sure it's supposed to be higher than this."

"Can I see?" We stopped right outside the doors. It was windy, a bad day to wear a dress, but she wore hers beautifully. I offered her my jacket to tie around her waist, but she shook her head.

I looked at her phone, seeing the copy of her paycheck. She was getting paid less than I was, but that wasn't what struck me the most.

"Mia Olive Sablan," I read. "Your name is Mia?"

"Yeah."

"Why don't people call you that?"

"I don't know. I've just always gone by Ollie even though it's a weird nickname." She scratched the back of her head, giggling.

I nodded. "You mind if I call you Mia?"

"Not at all. Go for it."

Looking her up and down, I thought she looked like

one. "Okay, Mia," I started. "Go talk to Shelly in the office. She'd know if your paycheck is higher or if it's right."

She said she'd head there before she went home.

"Cool. Awesome." I nodded, taking in the sight of her. She was a gorgeous person, one of those people who seemed to grow lovelier the more you know them, even if she wasn't the best cook around. I must have looked like an idiot when I realized how long I had been staring and a wave of embarrassment pushed me to get my keys and say goodbye. But once I took a step, I heard her call out.

"Um. Can I have your number? You know, just in case, I gotta ask you stuff. . . for work," she said in a timid voice that made my pulse run. It was surprising. She wanted to keep talking to me.

"Sure." I tried to fight the grin on my face, because I knew I'd look like an idiot (again) to her if I didn't. It was difficult as I gave her my phone number, but I managed to do it.

On my way to the truck, my phone buzzed with a text message from an unsaved number.

This is Mia:)

I brought the pizza box out with me to the lookout in Maina. I planted myself on the ledge, feeling the warmth of the sun. My stomach gurgled, but as I reached for a slice, something in me forced my appetite to cease. I realized that I hadn't eaten in days. My appetite was gone. And by the look of the sun hitting the skin on my forearms, I had lost the enjoyment of the sun's warmth.

I tried to regain it, but as minutes passed, I knew I wasn't going to get it back tonight. I wasn't sure if I was going to get that feeling back for a long while, so there was no point in staying.

I stood up on the ledge, and before I turned back to the car, I heard that wretched woman's voice. Hannah's voice. "So you're dating other girls at this time, huh, Veo?"

My brain felt like it clenched at the sound of her voice. Why was she still here? Did she move here? I heard she moved back to Seattle months ago, so why the hell was she back? Forget it. I didn't want to know. She was already my ex on paper. Now, of all times, wasn't one she was welcomed in.

I avoided her gaze, moving hastily to my dad's pick-up. I opened the driver's side door, but she slammed it shut. "Veo, who was that chick at that pizza place? Are you seeing her or what?"

Do not answer. Holy crap. Do not answer.

"Can't talk again? Probably because you know you'll mess up with her too like you did with me. So what is it, Veo? You with that whore?"

I was seething at this point, trying to hold back. If a single sound were to come out of my mouth, then she'd be around for the rest of the night, filling me up with unpleasantry. I pulled up any memories or stories or thoughts of any kind that would distract me from this woman. Anything at all. But all that came up was the memory of yesterday.

"What time is the appointment?" Dominic asked as he came out of Dad's room.

"We'll leave when Matthew gets here from work. He has the car."

Dominic nodded and started cleaning up the living room as I sat by the computer table. I was trying to draw whatever came to mind in an empty notebook that I found in one of my drawers. It was difficult to be creative at that point because my thoughts were grim. But I wanted to push them away and draw something epic. I sat for a while before being struck by an idea that shot me upright to sort it out. Once the point of the pencil touched the paper to start, Dad yelled out, calling for me or Dominic.

Dominic and I got up at the same time, but I signaled for him to sit back down. "I'll take care of it," I said, aware that I had just referred to Dad as an "it"—a chore rather than a person. It wasn't something that I wanted to think of him as, but the truth of my thoughts seemed to be cementing itself, regardless of my rational understanding that Dad was still a person.

He was groaning in pain, asking for any medicine that could counter this agony. I told him what the doctor said—that we could only use that pain medication after a set number of hours. It had only been three hours since he took it last.

He continued groaning even as I massaged his body. But in time, he fell back into the state that anyone who was sick or depressed wished to be in. Slumber. I made my way back to the living room, back to the computer table. My drawing set-up was untouched, but I couldn't remember what it was that I wanted to draw. A dragon? An anime-style hero? I scratched my head, trying to remember, but eventually gave up. All I knew was that it was something epic.

I sat back down, feeling a breeze enter the house like it always did on windy days. But it didn't feel the same. This room felt different. There were times when Dad would walk around with ease. But now, anything that he did was related to the cancer. Everything he talked about was too. There was no talk about building the next barbecue pit or assembling a new dish rack that hung on the walls by the sink. There were no discussions past asking us how our days were. I couldn't even tell if he could hear how we responded. And there were no requests to watch his sunset anymore.

With his attention solely on the pain, I couldn't think of a time when I'd be able to talk to him about the past. Maybe that time had passed already. Maybe I'd lost the opportunity to patch things up.

His groaning sounded nearby. I must have missed Matthew's arrival, because he was holding Dad up over his shoulder, and Dominic picked up Dad's other arm.

"The keys," Matthew said as I picked up their wallets and a bag. They crossed the living room and went out the screen door. But before I grabbed the keys, I studied Dad. He was barely able to stand and walk, and his head had given up trying to look up. There was almost no effort put into getting out the door. The pain he was going through held him back from accomplishing the most basic of tasks that even a toddler could do.

Dad. . . I thought as hard as I could, hoping that he'd somehow hear my thoughts, because the words would never come out my mouth. *Please walk. Please pick yourself up and walk.*

I waited for some miracle to happen where he would suddenly stop, stand up straight, and tell my brothers that he could head to the car on his own. But it didn't happen. With his ability to walk and talk gone, he might as well have dropped dead right then.

I slapped my face, telling myself that that was a horrible thing to think about. I felt my chest inhale and exhale as I took deeper breaths. The stress on my forehead was heavy as I threw my head back. "What the hell, Veo," I muttered to myself. "Dad's going to be okay. It's just a phase." But somewhere deep inside, I knew that it wasn't true.

By the time that we got to the clinic, it didn't take long for the doctor to tell us what my dad's status was.

"Your dad has entered the first stage of dying," Dr. Sonia said.

BANG! Hannah kicking my dad's pick-up brought me back to the present. She pulled back her leg, revealing a small dent that wasn't there a second ago. She'd hit my dad's car. The car he used to lift as if he were Superman. The car he drove my brothers and me around when we were kids. Now there was a dent on it. I felt my muscles tighten as I looked her dead in the eyes.

"Don't you fuckin' hit my dad's car."

She froze, struck silent at my serious tone. She was searching somewhere in her for a response, but I wasn't having it. "Don't you dare fuckin' hit it," I said again.

I got into the pick-up and rolled up my windows, trying to forget about this stupid girl. Girls shouldn't be a big part of my life, but they were entering it as if this was their only chance. All these times in my life, like high school, and only now was when girls wanted me.

What the fuck.

What the fuck.

WHAT THE FUCK.

I started to scream inside the car until I was hitting my head against the steering wheel, hoping for some kind of pain to make me forget what was going on with Dad. How the pick-up wasn't being driven by him anymore. How I could predict his word of the day would be "medicine." How I could hear his groans and grunts, fresh in my head because that was all I was hearing from him. How he wasn't asking for a beer or to be taken outside to watch the sunset after a hard day's worth of work. And how I still heard that doctor saying that he had entered the first fucking stage of dying.

It was all something I wasn't ready for.

I must have sat there for a long time, in his pick-up. I cooled down over time, but the pain was still fresh. I wished that Hannah would leave me alone at that point, that she'd never return to this island, that she'd move back to Seattle or California or wherever the hell she wanted that wasn't here. Now wasn't the time to get with girls. But she just sat on the ledge of the look-out with a concerned look on her face. I lost track of time, feeling every second hit me with a pulse of reality that I was going to lose someone. I muttered curse words under my breath before I checked the time on my phone. It was 10:00 p.m. I took a deep breath before I started the pick-up. The loud engine must have pushed Hannah to stand up and walk over to my window. I didn't want to talk to her, but she seemed sane enough right now, so I rolled down the window and waited for her to say whatever she needed to say.

"This is the last time I'll visit."

I nodded, saying nothing.

"I hope your dad gets better, Veo."

I felt my grip on the steering wheel tighten, hearing those words of pity from an ex I never wanted to see again.

"I hope things work out with that girl too," she lightly chuckled, but my jaw clenched. "Goodbye," she said before she started for her rental car.

I took a deep breath. Figuring that this was truly the last time I'd see her, I honked the horn. Hannah looked back at me. The muscles of my face tensed as I pulled every bit of my being together to be kind to her in some way. But I did it. I felt myself relax as I lifted my arm and waved goodbye to her. She gave a soft smile before she dropped her gaze down to the rocky road and headed back to her car. The last time I ever saw her.

TRACK #16
I'll Be That

When I was 7 years old. . .

"*UMBIYA*! WHAT HAPPENED to my eggplant?" Dad said once he opened the fridge, followed by some mutterings that I couldn't make out. He had picked me up from the airport. I actually flew by myself. Me, a seven-year-old, flew by myself. I took a lot of pride in that.

Matthew and Dominic's faces lit up once they saw Dad walk in carrying my things with me trailing behind. Dominic was excited to see me and Matthew's eyes twinkled with amazement at my accomplishment of flying by myself. I may as well have been piloting the airplane. Of course, Dad kept it from me for years that I was actually flying with my aunt who I never got to know. I only saw her at rosaries, family parties, and festivals. But I only thought of her as a distant relative that I had to amen. I didn't even talk to her on the plane. She only sat next to me, so it was safe to consider that trip a solo adventure.

"What was it like? Were you scared?" Matthew asked. But before I could answer, Dad stepped in, asking who ate his eggplant. Matthew looked confused, but Dominic spoke up, "It was Uncle Dun. He came in, and asked us for them, then he left."

Dad rubbed his forehead, muttering something again that I couldn't make out. He then motioned my brothers out the screen door. Dominic yelled that he needed his school bag and Matthew followed suit. Once they grabbed their bags, they hugged me before disappearing out the door with Dad.

I stood in the middle of the living room, taking in the smell of freshly cooked eggs and bacon that was left for me. The smell of Dad's cigarette ashes in the ashtray, the wooden walls, and the lavender scent of some cleaning chemical, used to clean the entire house also lingered. My home here wasn't grand. It was simple, and it was enough.

I ran and jumped on the couch, unsurprised but reminded of the small pinches of this cracked faux leather furniture. It didn't bother me though, because I'd missed having strong, worn-down furniture that could stand me running on top of it. Dominic and I liked to wrestle on top of the back cushions. We'd push each other until the other fell on the bottom cushion. The one left standing would then claim the title "Champion of the World!" I didn't have that on Saipan. Friends, or brothers. Everyone was older than me and wanted to play cards all the time or talk. Getting the "Champion of the World" title wasn't exactly fun if there was nobody there to challenge me for it.

The thought of my brothers coming back after school was exciting. The Mafnas Men and the Man had reunited! Everything else were additional points added to my life, making it even better. Everything looked like it did before I left, especially the window view of the ocean by the couch. The day view was as pretty as the night. Maybe I was too young to be struck by how beautiful a place was, but I didn't care. No matter how old I am, when I remember that view, I hear the waves pushing against the sand on the beach and the sound of the coconut tree leaves brushing against each other. It is a sound that I never want to forget.

The screen door opened and shut, followed by Dad telling me to get ready. We had to shop for my school supplies because I started school next week. I happily got down, and went to my brothers' bedroom, where I would also be sleeping from now on. I was changing my clothes and thinking about where I could put my things when Dad came in asking, "Son, you haven't eaten yet?"

"No."

"Why?"

"Because I'm not hungry. You could give it to Matthew and Dominic when they come back."

"But they already," he paused before getting on his knees. "Veo, the food will be cold by then, and you will get hungry later. You have to eat."

"But Dad, I—"

"Son," he interrupted, "We don't have a lot of money. You have to eat it. I'm not going to cook you anything two hours from now just because you didn't eat breakfast."

He walked out and I followed him to the table and ate. I thought I was in trouble, so I kept quiet, but I reflected on what he said.

We really didn't have a lot of money.

But a smile came on my face when I thought of a

solution. Dad then asked me why I was smiling, and I decided to make it a surprise.

"Nothing. Just thinking of something funny," I lied. But he knew I was a bad liar. He just didn't fight it.

FOR MY FIRST week of school back on Guam, I didn't talk much. I couldn't bring myself to say anything to anyone. I even heard Mrs. Johnson asking Dad if this was normal for me. She suggested that I be placed in a special education class, but he told her to wait it out. He said I was a loud kid and right now, I was only shy. I suppose I was shy, but I had nothing to talk about and no games or toys to play with the others. Everyone else liked different things. It was okay though. I spent a lot of my time in school thinking of my brothers and Dad and my special project, which was already a week in.

It was Friday when I got home with the brothers and Dad after school and I saw Uncle Dun hanging out by the front of the house. The man hadn't changed much. He was still bald and the same shade of brown he had always been. It was as if he stood under the sun all day long like he was a construction worker. He wore his dark sunglasses, the ones that made him look like he was blind. His clothing was the same as it was before. There was no style to it, and I wasn't surprised. He never dressed to impress. He wore clothes so he wouldn't get a ticket from officers for nudity. I remember him saying that if nudity wasn't a law, then his closet wouldn't have anything in it. Dad shot me with a look once he heard my giggling at Uncle Dun's joke, which I soon figured wasn't a joke at all. Uncle Dun said a lot of funny things, but it usually had the truth in them. That was why I liked having him around.

"Hey, Little Man," he said as he stood from the foldable chair. I hugged him once I reached him. "Couldn't keep away from home, huh?" he asked, pinching my nose.

I laughed as my brothers rushed into the house, yelling about their *Yu-Gi-Oh* cards. Their cards were no match for me though. Although both Dominic and Matthew were worthy opponents, Matthew didn't like to read the cards before placing it down. He relied on the status of the hits and defenses. Same went for Dominic. This didn't stop me from joining them though. I ran into the house and grabbed my deck.

"I challenge you to a duel!" Matthew said, holding his deck out at me in our bedroom. Before I said anything, I heard Dad yelling outside. We all looked out the window behind the curtain to see him angry, muffling things that we couldn't hear him say. Uncle Dun stood there as calm as ever, listening to his brother scream. He laughed at Dad before I heard Dad clearly yell, "Leave!"

Uncle Dun didn't fight it. He shook his head as he got in his pick-up and left. Dad was still angry but frozen until he glanced at the window at us. We quickly hid behind the curtain. It was too late though. I heard the screen door slam and his footsteps on the hollow floor. He was in the bedroom by the count of three. Matthew and I were standing and staring at him, waiting for him to say something. Dominic hid beneath the blanket, pretending to sleep.

"Dominic, get up. I know you're awake."

Dominic stayed still for a second before pretending to yawn and stretch. "Hi, Dad."

"Go next to your brothers."

Dominic looked down as he stood next to us.

"Have you boys been egging the neighbors?"

All three of us scattered looks at each other, confused.

"Look at me when I'm talking to you," Dad said with his nostrils flaring. We all looked at him before he repeated the question. "Have you boys been egging Auntie Connie and Joseph Reyes' house? Tell me the truth."

His eyes scanned me, then Matthew, then Dominic. We all shook our heads.

"Don't lie to me. We're missing a whole carton of eggs and they told me their houses got egged."

Matthew spoke up, "Maybe the eggs were already finished when it happened. Did you eat them, Dad?"

"Just answer the question, boys. Did you use the eggs?"

"No, Dad," we all answered.

He stood up straight and nodded before leaving the room. Fear crossed my brothers' faces as they talked to each other, wondering what happened to the eggs. I faced the wall, hiding the grimace that I couldn't suppress. I knew where the eggs were. Maybe the missing eggs were why he was yelling at Uncle Dun. Crap.

I looked out the window at the neighbors' houses. Auntie Connie's house was right next to ours and Joseph's was across the road. The houses didn't look like they'd been egged. But then I realized that I was only seeing one side of their houses.

I LOVE MANGO season. It's like that duck season vs. rabbit season argument that Bugs Bunny and Daffy Duck had, where whatever season it was, it was the time focused on collecting that particular animal for consumption. Mango season was the time of year when they dropped from trees. Sometimes they would have holes in them, because the birds got to them before they made it to the ground. But sometimes they would drop without holes. They were never good for me though, so one day, I copied what Dad did on the days of non-mango season. I took a long stick and poked at the mangos until they dropped. No holes and almost as solid as a rock. Perfection. Dad told me that ripe mangos are supposed to be softer and squishier than that, but those types of mangos always tasted too sweet. If he wanted a super sweet treat, he should have gone to the store and bought candy. To me, mangos are supposed to be sour and sweet at the same time.

On top of that, though, Dad taught me and my brothers how to plant a mango tree. It all begins with a mango. We had to eat it as best as we could, dig a hole in the soil, and bury the eaten mangos there. Of course, we would have to water it every day, but it was that easy. After a while, green sprouted from the ground where we saw Dad plant the mango. It was then that he told me that I could plant many vegetables and fruits like that.

So there I was, hanging out by the hidden corner by the house where nobody really went with eggs and eggplants in my hands. Dominic, Matthew, and Dad had gone to the store for groceries. He was growing more and more frustrated with the food going missing. But I kept reminding myself that he would be happy when we had so many eggplants growing in the back that he wouldn't ever have to buy eggplants again. I planned on doing this with string beans and avocados too, but for now, only eggplants.

I dug several holes in the ground and planted the remaining eggs in them and the last eggplant. I figured that Dad wouldn't notice when he came home with groceries, so I smiled. I could feel the eggs that I'd planted a week ago growing and I knew that they'd be sprouting soon. I only had to have patience.

When I finished, they returned. I ran to the car to help with the groceries. Once we got in and placed the plastic bags in the kitchen, my brothers showed me the candies they got. When I asked for some, they both reached in and pulled out one piece of candy held by their thumb and index with their pinkies out, making sure that that was all I got. I put it in my mouth and held my hand open for another one in a flash. *Nice try, brothers.* But my moment with my brothers was cut short by Dad groaning about Uncle Dun stealing food again, particularly the eggs.

"This guy doesn't know how to ask. He just has to wait until I leave. What is he doing with the eggs? Building a fort of them?" He threw his arms up and headed out with the plastic bags still on the floor.

I turned my attention back to my brothers as I waited for more candy. Matthew ran off to the bedroom, but Dominic stayed, giving me a few more pieces.

"Is Dad mad?" I asked. But our conversation was cut short by our curiosity at the yelling outside. Dominic and I ran out to the screen door to listen. It was Dad and Uncle Dun again.

"Stop stealing my food!"

"I'm not stealing your food. I told you a million times—"

"No! No! I know it's you!"

"What? Did I leave my business card in there? Why are you—"

"Dammit, Dun! You've always taken my things. Get a job! Get your own food!"

"Ey. Come on. What kind of brother—"

"What kind of brother what?!"

The conversation went on until I saw Dad turn around, light a branch on fire, and throw it into the jungle followed by some curse words that I was taught not to say at that age. My heart was beating fast. Was this worth a surprise of a new garden? I ran outside to Dad, but Uncle Dun got a hold of me while his back was turned. Smoke grew darker and darker as my pulse grew and grew. I needed to say something, to reveal my surprise, anything.

My mind was racing until I heard Uncle Dun laugh as if this was nothing. "*Ai*, my little brother," he laughed, shaking his head.

We stood there as Dad continued to burn the jungle.

EVERYTHING HAD SETTLED down. Uncle Dun had gone home, and the jungle fire was put out. I couldn't sleep that night though. I kept thinking that my surprise garden for

Dad would be the reason why he stopped talking to Uncle Dun and caused the death of the jungle and all its animals and birds. It was all my fault. What if the jungle police officers found out that it was Dad that set everything on fire? He might go to prison. I wouldn't get to see him for a long time, nor would my brothers. *It was all my fault*, I thought as I lay down on the futon.

My brothers were still asleep on their bunk beds. Day was beginning to break from the change in light I saw from the curtained window. Then I heard footsteps from the kitchen. Dad must be up, and I knew for sure that he was when I heard one of his songs playing. I kept listening as I tried to calm myself down.

Oh, Baby, if you want me to be your singer
If you want me to be your light
If you want me to be your creature
Filling your silent nights just right

If you want me to be your one
Your man, your partner in crime
Then tell me and in an instant
I'll be that, I'll be yours for all time

I finally mustered the courage and got up. *I'm going to tell him*, I thought. I made my way out of the bedroom and across the kitchen. He didn't seem to notice my loud footsteps as he smoked by the window.

"Dad?"

He turned around and blew out a stream of smoke

before putting the cigarette out and saying, "You're up early."

He looked up at me. My eyebrows knitted once my eyes met his, pushing him to ask me if I was okay. I nodded.

I was trying to find the words to tell him about my surprise garden for him, but my body felt like it was being chained along with my voice. Once I opened my mouth, fear got a hold of my words. "I think I should stay with Mom," I said.

He stared at me, surprised. It felt like a moment that stood for minutes that could have just been a second. He held out his arm, motioning for me to come closer, and so I did. "Why do you want to stay with Mom?"

I didn't answer. I didn't know how to answer. I knew I didn't want to move back to Saipan. The words only came out like that. "Son?" he asked.

My eyes got glossy. Crap. I was supposed to be a big boy. Why was I crying? I took a deep breath before telling him, "I tried to plant a garden for you." My vision was blurring, but I could see Dad smiling as he asked, "Really? Where'd you plant it?"

I pointed to the window that the garden was next to. He then got up, pulled my hand, and we went out to the garden. Did he want to see my progress? I grew hopeful that maybe my surprise was a good thing, and that this would patch everything up. But I was still fighting back tears.

"Where is it?"

I pointed to the area and walked over. "It's a garden of eggplants, Dad."

He smiled with a lifted brow. "Where'd you get the eggplants seeds?"

I grew nervous before I opened my mouth, wondering if he was going to get mad. But I knew that I couldn't hide it anymore. "I took the eggs from the fridge."

He furrowed his eyebrows with the smile still on his face. If anything, his smile looked like it grew. "What?" he asked.

"I used the eggs from the fridge. It's an eggplant, Dad."

He then shook his head and laughed. It was so contagious that I eventually joined in. "You can't grow eggplants from eggs, son."

"Why not? It's an eggplant."

"Because they're chicken eggs," he said. "*Ai Adai*. My son and my brother."

He went on to teach me how to plant eggplants. My stupidity had set him in a happy mood for the rest of the day. By the time we were heading back into the house, he was still smiling. I, on the other hand, dropped my head low, remembering that I wasted eighteen eggs for my failed attempt at an eggplant garden. "I'm sorry, Dad."

"Don't be sorry, son. You had good intentions."

"But I'm the reason why you got mad at Uncle Dun and why you burned the jungle down." I dropped my head again, feeling my eyes welling up once more at the incoming thoughts that were worsening at what I had done. "And those animals and birds lost their home because of me."

There were steps that led to the front screen door. I was behind him as he stepped onto them, but he sat on the top and patted my head. "Is that why you want to go back to your mom?" he asked.

I looked somewhere else. I didn't know what I was looking at, I only knew who I *wasn't* looking at. I felt embarrassed. I was supposed to be the oldest one. The most responsible one.

"Veo, if you want to go back to Saipan, then I'll send you with Uncle Pete. He's flying there tomorrow. But you should know that both me and your mom think you should stay here, because you're the oldest one. Your brothers missed you and I know you missed them." I looked at him.

"And I missed you also, son. You're going to make a lot of mistakes. But it's best that you have your brothers and me here to witness it and laugh about it later on." He put his large hand on my shoulder. "Just like your eggplant garden," he laughed before I joined in.

"So do you still want to go back?" he asked.

I couldn't help myself. I threw my arms around him and said, "No, Dad. I want to stay here."

"Good."

I pulled away, and he got up and went in to start breakfast. I stood outside for a little bit, trying to soak in my throbbing heart that was going through a rollercoaster of emotions.

"And don't be planting any more chicken eggs, Veo," I heard him say. He went on replaying "I'll Be That" on the cassette player speakers.

"I won't waste any more chicken eggs, Dad."

TRACK #17
Have You Heard Your Name

When I was 23 years old. . .

THIS SONG WAS playing off the TV in the living room while I sat on the toilet. Then I heard Auntie Connie's voice from outside. "Daniel! Dominic! Veo—" she shouted only to be greeted by Matthew, who was the only other one awake in the house this early in the morning. I finished up my business, finding her outside surprisingly with Val and Riri.

"Hi," Val greeted me nervously, holding Riri's hand.

"Hi," I said before turning my attention to Auntie Connie. I bowed to her after Matthew.

"How's your dad?" she asked, heading inside with her plastic bag of gauze, alcohol, and other things. She visited every day just to check up on us all, and she always looked so concerned especially since Dad was her last sibling alive. While my brothers and I felt heavy because it was our dad that was sick, I couldn't imagine how she felt, losing another brother.

She and Matthew went inside. I decided to stay outside with Val and Riri, but the air between us was growing too uncomfortable, so I asked them if they wanted to come inside to watch TV instead.

Val shook her head. "I, uh, actually wanted to see you," she said. She was fidgeting with her nails as her daughter looked around.

"Okay. Well, how are you?" I asked.

"I'm good," she said before she pulled herself together and asked if Riri could go inside so we could talk privately. I nodded, then I brought the little one into the kitchen to be with her Uncle Matthew.

"So what'd you want to talk about?" I asked when I came back out.

"My dad passed away a couple of years ago. I'm sure you remember. He really loved you guys."

"Yeah. I remember. I'm sorry."

"No, no. I'm sorry. I just. . . I guess I came over to see how you were doing. We don't have the best relationships with our dads, but it doesn't make it hurt any less since they were still there."

"Right. I'm okay though." I nodded. Val wasn't someone I was going to open up to, and by the look on her face, I could tell she knew I didn't trust her. She scratched her head and let her eyes wander the area. I felt the conversation coming to an end until she opened her mouth. "I'm sorry, Veo. I know I screwed you over before, making you think Riri was yours and that we did something. But honestly, I just. . . something had to happen for my dad to pay attention. And I was right."

Her eyes were wide and bright after saying something so twisted. I furrowed my eyebrows, waiting for her to go on.

"I just wish that I had more time with him, and I know that you wish the same thing with your dad too. And well, I just came over to apologize." Her eyes dropped before locking onto mine where we stood still for a while, feeling the breeze blow on the spots where our dads would argue like the siblings they were.

There was no point into holding on to these feelings that I barely thought of these days, so I nodded, hoping that she'd catch my way of saying that all was forgiven. By her soft smile, I could tell she caught on.

"Riri isn't my daughter though, right?" I broke the silence with a question I had to make sure I had the answer to.

Val laughed and shook her head. "We really didn't do anything, cuz."

"Good," I said. "Wanna come in?"

"Sure." She smiled, successfully resetting our relationship before she stepped foot in the house. I wondered then if our relationship could ever be as close as Dad was to Uncle Dun. Maybe we'd be drinking beer in the garage someday. Hopefully, we would.

THE NEXT DAY, I woke up on the kitchen floor. The tiles felt cold when I lay down on it in the morning. The sun must have been coming up at that moment, but since the day I'd gone on that pizza run, I hadn't been thinking of watching the sun's activity. According to my elementary teachers, I wasn't supposed to be looking directly at it either, because

I'd be killing my eyesight. But all my childhood, I tested that fact with my theory that the sun only strengthened my eyes. It was simply a workout for them. That was silly child-me.

At some points of the day, the cold kitchen's hollow floor was actually welcoming. I would hear my brothers' footsteps as they walked across the room as I escaped the heat from outside. But on this day, I lay down regardless of the abnormally chilly weather outside. It was also a day that my dad's pain was inescapable even for me and my brothers. Lying down on that kitchen floor was the calmest point.

I heard his groaning from the kitchen, signaling the start of my day. I got up, making my footsteps as heavy as possible to let my brothers know that they could go back to sleep. I shut the door behind me, before trying to figure out which part of his body was hurting. By this time, I had already adjusted to a ritual of massaging him, starting with his arm, working down to his hands, then his shoulders, his back, his butt, his thighs, calves, feet, then back upward. But my dad pointed to the door before I touched him and muttered, "Toilet."

I helped him up, and as I walked him to the bathroom, I recalled the beginning of this whole process. When the pain started to take a toll on his movements, I'd only assist him to the bathroom and stand by the door, waiting for him to finish his business. But we had gone past that point.

I held him steady as he squatted to sit on the toilet. There were times where he told me that he didn't need that kind of help. But then one time, I found him on the floor, struggling to rid himself of pain instead of getting up from his puddle of urine. That was enough for me not to listen to him anymore about what he could handle with the toilet.

I brought him back to the bedroom where he knocked out instantly. I covered him with the blanket before leaving, finding Dominic up, prepping and cooking breakfast. Throughout the rest of the day, whenever Dad called out for help or the time for medications arrived, we switched turns going in as we usually did like any other day.

But as night fell, my turn came up again for medication. I entered the room with a cup of water. As I helped him sit up, I saw the pillow under his head decorated with little bits of liquid. After giving him his medicines, I switched out his pillows and wondered as I massaged him back to sleep what caused it. Was something leaking out of his ears? Did Matthew or Dominic spill something on the pillow? But as I reached my last theory, I remembered how strong this guy was, lifting cars up, bush-cutting the yard to perfection, assembling different things together for projects to improve the house, driving that worn-down pick-up that forced him to stop at the side of the road multiple times, going to the jungle for firewood to avoid buying charcoal. There had been so many painful scenarios that he put himself through, but they had never resulted in tears.

Once I figured his pain had ceased for the moment, I stood up only to have my dad reach for my wrist. He froze silently, not saying anything, but his face hinted at regret. His droopy eyes were slightly open, and I waited for some signal of where his pain was, but I didn't see any. I placed myself in his position, figuring that maybe he was lonely. Lying in a room alone in pain for months wasn't an exciting way to live, so I sat back down beside the bed and held onto his hands until he slept again.

I made my way to the living room, finding my brothers asleep on the couches. It felt like it was early in the night, and I was right. It was only 8:14 p.m. Setting the futon on the floor, I watched the intro of a movie and fell asleep before it finished.

My sleep that night though was broken once I felt a heavy thud vibrating through the floor. Surveying the area once I got up, I knew it wasn't anything in the kitchen or living room. I made my way to Dad's bedroom and found him on the floor, trying to get up but failing. I held him by his arms, asking if he was okay.

"Yeah. . . yeah. . . yeah. . ."

"Come on. Let's get you back to bed."

"Outside."

"What? No, it's dark outside, and it's too cold."

"Outside. . . outside. . ." His voice tried to sound stern as he continued. "Outside. . . Now, son."

It was 5:02 a.m. Not an ideal time to be outside, but since it wouldn't be dark for too long, I helped him up.

Grabbing a blanket, we made our way past the front door and screen door. I sat him down on one of the white chairs that he and Uncle Dun sat in during their beer times, watching the sunsets. But it still felt all foreign to me, especially after I wrapped him in a blanket.

I took a seat across him, my back to the sunrise. Once I settled down, I asked him if he was okay. All he said was to move my chair next to him. When I did so, I found us facing the horizon that was barely visible.

We sat in silence. Thinking that maybe he wanted to

get out of the bedroom, I accepted hanging out with my dad before the day began. It was supposed to feel pleasant. But this view wasn't doing anything for me. I only felt an uncomfortable tingling in my stomach, but I tried to shake it off. Telling myself to shut up and not remember this moment, I shook my head until my dad asked me, "Do you remember. . . Tito?"

I glanced up before shooting my gaze down, and I felt my heartbeat. Not faster or slower, but harder. It had been years since I heard that name. "I do."

He took a deep breath. I had been hoping for a time to talk to him about this stuff, and I wasn't expecting it to feel this way, like this topic was so far gone that if it was physically manifested into anything, it'd be a housefly. And because I didn't know if that fly would actually hold a solution, I didn't try to catch it.

But he did.

"I'm. . . sorry. . . son."

For years, I didn't know what I wanted from him. Every time those memories surfaced, I pushed them to the back of my mind. But I sat there, trying to contain myself. I knew that if anything came out of my mouth, the words would break and so would my tear ducts. I turned to face him. Just like the little bits of light that were breaking out, shining onto him and everything around us, so were the grudges that I pulled from the corners of my mind, letting them disappear with the darkness.

I only nodded, hoping that he understood, that he caught on. By the way the corners of his mouth curved, I could tell that he heard that one message that mattered the most.

He turned to the sunrise. "Take. . . care. . . of. . . your brothers."

"I will."

I watched the sunrise with him, noticing how fast it moved when it made an appearance. I always thought of sunrises as a surfacing of jobs and duties that needed to be unloaded in the next twelve hours. That was why I always preferred sunsets.

As if he had heard me, Dad said one of the things that still lingers in my head today. "There's always. . . another. . . way. . . to. . . enjoy life."

He shot me a look, and before I could question him on whether he could possibly read minds, he asked me to play him a tune.

"You want the radio? I can play from your car—"

"Guitar. . . You play."

It was an odd request, but I got the guitar from the living room. I tuned it, since it'd been sitting under the computer table for a couple of years now. I asked him what song he wanted to hear.

He was calm, the most content that I've seen him in a long time. "Anything. . . Whatever comes to mind," he coughed.

The first song that comes to mind, I mused. And in an instant, I knew what to play. Messing around with the strings at first, I made sure that the guitar was right for the tune that I knew my dad loved to hear. I began singing once I could tell he recognized the tune.

Have you heard your name
That whistling tune in the river

Somehow it rings the same
If said with a shout or a shiver
When I meet death, my final breath
Will slowly spill your name with a quiver

The song continued in me and I could tell that my dad wanted to sing along but wanting to hear the song more, he sealed his mouth, content with listening to his son play one of his favorite songs.

I strummed the last string, trying to remember every aspect of this moment that I had previously tried to force away from imprinting in my memories. I put the guitar away, aware that the moment was fleeting the higher the sun traveled.

I exhaled, wishing that time would freeze so I wouldn't worry about my dad getting even sicker. I knew that each day would get worse for him, and it'd be difficult for me and my brothers to stand in the same room with him. But at that moment, I remembered what my dad said a few minutes ago, that there was always another way to enjoy things.

The moment I realized what he meant, he opened his mouth and asked what he always asked before. "I'm. . . still. . . listening. . . How's your day?"

I smiled. "It just started, Dad."

THE DAYS OF the next few weeks, he was in immense pain. But there were also days where he fought the pain, letting it travel to the back of his mind as a minor thing in life. There was one day where I was in his room. I entered to find him getting off the bed, latching on to the dresser, the walls, the door, and everything within reach to make it to the living room on his own. His ability to stand on his own improved. The sense of hope was growing in me, and I forgot why I even came in the room until I looked at his medicines in my hands.

"Dad! You need to take your medicine!" I called out, knowing that maybe they were kicking in in an extreme way and helping Dad get better. Maybe all he needed was time with the medications for him to run backward from the last stages of life.

I felt the corners of my mouth curve once I heard him tell my brothers to clean the living room in his commanding voice that he used before he got sick. It always ensured we did what he said. I watched as my brothers did what he said, noticing their shift from boredom with video games to upbeat at Dad's familiar admonition about house upkeep. I remember leaning on the wall, enjoying what was going on until Dad took notice of me.

"Veo, give me those medicines. . . and help your brothers with this mess. *Ai*! It's like. . . you guys didn't think I'd notice this."

I felt my body straighten up like a soldier, like I did when I was a kid before all these things happened between us. My body relaxed as soon as I smiled once I remembered my child self, and I handed him his medicine with a cup of water from the kitchen.

As I swept the floor of the living room, he took a seat by the computer table. "Matthew. . . what's for lunch?"

Matthew was used to cooking whatever was in the kitchen, so he was interrupted once he suggested frying spam with Dad saying, "*Ai. Umbiya*. Fry some fish. . . Dominic, go to the store. . . and get some fish. . . . And Veo. . ."

"Yes, sir," I answered playfully.

"Keep cleaning."

"On it!"

Afterward, I laughed at my brothers before they got to their task of the day, like I did when I was a kid. Of course, I was aware that maybe today was one where the pain was the most tolerable for Dad, that maybe the pain would get much worse as the days went on. I felt a drop in my chest once that thought surfaced, only to remind myself that even if it was only temporary, which I hoped it wasn't, it was still a good day to have. I wasn't going to let negative thoughts of the future ruin that one good day.

I got the place spotless, even doing the extra task of getting the mop we hadn't used since we bought it to disinfect and shine the hollow floor. The house smelled of mouth-watering tilapia that Matthew seasoned to perfection. Lunch that day consisted of me, Matthew, Dominic, and Dad sitting at the dining table like we did before he got sick. But there was nothing between me and Dad that hindered me from enjoying that lunch, making it a meal to remember.

Matthew went on defending his college of choice, which we all knew was because Kayla couldn't get into his top schools. Dominic admitted that after high school, he wanted to move to Seattle because he knew I was there, but he had no regrets going to Indiana. He was probably the most successful of us all even though all our lives were put on halt right now.

As if Dad was thinking the same, I caught his eyelids sagging as they dropped to the table. My brothers caught onto it too, and silence fell. But Dad quickly picked himself up and noticing that I wasn't saying anything about what was happening with me, he brought it up. Of course, there was nothing new happening with me other than him dying, but that wasn't something to talk about on a good day. There was also Mia, who I hadn't texted. But I knew that even if I did date her, we might end up like Matthew and Kayla. It'd be a bad mix that should be cut off early in the relationship. That was a last memory of me that I didn't want Dad to have.

"Anything? Anything. . . new at work? . . . New hobby? . . . New girlfriend?"

I shook my head, saying, "Nope. Just a boring guy on Guam."

"Well then, what was living in Seattle like?" Dominic asked. And from there, we branched off into the world of traveling, my life in Seattle, how Matthew was liking it here, why Dad traveled to Japan each year before he had us, which was the most surprising of all.

I had never looked at him as a traveler until he talked about it that day. He told us about Japan's culture of respect, the whole other world of art and cartoons that he didn't watch but admired, and the cherry blossoms that bloomed and scattered on green, creating the most beautiful natural color scheme. I could only imagine how beautiful the country was by his stories. At the end of his stories, I imagined hearing the breeze blow against the pink trees as he lay on the grass underneath with the flowers swaying back and forth overhead. At that point, I could only wonder where else he had been. But mostly, it made me wonder why he stayed on Guam.

Dominic stood up, collecting our empty plates. After two hours, lunch was coming to a close. "So, Dad," he started. "There's this movie that I want you to watch."

"Yeah? . . . What's it called?"

"*The Soldier in the Jungle.*" Dominic was already by the TV, sorting through whatever was in a plastic bag that he must have brought home when he got the tilapia. "I think you'll like it," he said before he explained that the movie was about a World War II soldier.

"Well, play it," Dad said, coughing, before getting up slowly to walk to the couch. Thinking that maybe he needed help, I reached out for his arm. But he raised his palm, telling me to either wait or that he had this in the bag. I was hoping for the latter. By the time he reached the couches and sat down, I knew that my hope was like a professional tightrope walker doing their thing, only the walker was running. Running with the thrill blocking the rational part of their brain shouting that they might fall. Feeling that they'd succeed, yes. But still a great chance that they'd fail existing.

We watched the movie once Matthew finished the dishes. At some point, Dominic tossed me popcorn from the plastic bag once he heard some stomach grumbling among us. I wondered who could have possibly still been hungry from that lunch but remembered that we sat around a table for two hours even after finishing our food. Just talking.

It was 5:36 p.m. when I finished with the popcorn. With the sun shining outside, I knew that it would set by the time the movie finished, which, like two wires finally connecting, made me realize that he'd like to see the sunset today too.

I sat back down, waiting and watching the movie, but by the time the 6 o'clock was nearing its end, I was tempted to pause the movie so he could watch the sunset. But as I was getting up, his attention was fully locked onto the screen, not even taking notice of movements around him.

"Dad?" I called, but he only responded with a low, "Yeah?" with his eyes still on the screen. He didn't sit still for many movies, but he was for this one. I smiled and sat comfortably, telling myself to enjoy the movie. "Never mind."

The sun was gone by the time the movie finished, but I didn't mind and neither did anyone else. The credits rolled up with a tune, triggering something in me. As I listened to the lyrics, which I normally didn't, I found one line that maybe, as stupid as I thought it was, was a sign from the universe. To believe in miracles.

Gazing at my dad and how much happier he was today, I couldn't help myself but hope.

"I like it. . . . It's a good. . . movie, son."

"Yeah? I knew you'd like it," Dominic said as he took out the disc. "So what next?" he asked.

Dad said that he was finished for the day.

"You don't look tired. You sure, Dad?" I asked.

"You. . . of all people. . . should know. . . that looks

don't. . . always match. . . the feelings, Veo." He smiled with a raised brow. "Help me up."

I extended a hand only for him to stand up and push my arm away as he latched onto nearby walls and furniture to help him into the bedroom. There was a tickle in my gut, forcing me to laugh.

"Laughing at. . . your dad, huh?" he asked.

"No, no, Dad. Not laughing at you."

"Right."

When we got to his room, he asked his usual question. "How was. . . your day?"

"You should know. I've been with you the whole day," I said, smiling as I brought out his medicine.

"Hey. . . was it. . . a good day. . . or what? That's all you. . . need to say, boy." He chuckled as I told him, "It was a very good day, Dad."

"Good."

I gave him his medicine, recounting the day until the Japan visits surfaced. I couldn't help myself but wonder. "Dad?"

"Yeah?" he asked after he drank water to flush the pills down.

"Why didn't you move to Japan or the mainland or any other country?"

He lay back down slowly with his eyes wandering, looking like he was trying to piece together his answer. I waited until the line of his mouth curved with his eyes resting on the ceiling.

"I don't know," he coughed. "I guess because the best stories. . . I could ever tell are ones. . . with people I love. And if I lived in a place. . . because of its beauty and nothing else. . . then that beauty would bore me. . . back to home base. Yes, this. . . Guam is my home base. . . . My friends, my family. . . and I'm lucky to have the place with. . . the most beautiful sunsets. . . as my home."

"You think Guam has the most beautiful sunsets?"

"Yeah. . . don't you?"

"I think the ones in Saipan are better."

"Well, son, . . . even if. . . it wasn't the best, it's still. . . amazing to watch every day."

I looked down, wondering if that was maybe what went wrong in Seattle. A beautiful place with things to do every day. But alone. "You know, Seattle was pretty amazing."

Dad's eyes were on me, waiting for more. If I continued on though, I'd be talking about Hannah. I cocked my head back and let myself breathe. "Do you have any regrets, Dad?"

"I do."

"Other than our relationship."

"I do. . . . I regret. . . letting your mom go. . . . She's one of those. . . rare women. . . that could keep me. . . smiling. . . . After all this time."

"Why don't you go get her?"

Dad sighed. The air in the room shifted heavy once I saw the lines on his forehead crease. The ticking of the clock on the wall grew louder, making its appearance on our situation. I knew what he was thinking. "It's not too—"

He waved his hand off, shaking his head. His eyes locked on mine as he gave me a reassuring smile. "Don't make the. . . same mistakes. . . I made. . . . Hannah. . . was just one girl. . . . Whatever woman. . . you choose to love. . . go all out."

I shook my head, dropping my gaze with a grin. "Now isn't the time for girls, Dad. I got you to worry about."

"Not for long." He reached for my hand. "Wherever life. . . takes you son. . . I hope. . . that you are never alone."

I felt locked in place, frozen. *Take a deep breath*, I told myself. But I couldn't even do that. I clenched my jaw once I saw a gentle smile grow on his face. Not taking it anymore, I did whatever I could that didn't make me sob. I hugged him as best as I could and told him what I hadn't said in years.

"I love you."

I felt his arm rub against my back. "I love you too, son."

I let go, and laughed a bit, trying to shake off the awkward moment. Dad could only smile at what I was doing. He knew how the room felt, but I knew from his experiences, he could only appreciate what was happening.

I headed toward the door and just before I was about to step out, I said, "Just let me know if you need anything, Dad."

"Where are you. . . going?"

I was about to ask him if he wanted to sleep when a thought crossed my mind. It was as if I had morphed into my child self and walked back to the chair by my dad's bed, readying myself not to listen, but to tell my dad stories to lull him to sleep like he did when I was a kid.

"So. . ." I began, not knowing what to tell him. He squinted at the ceiling like he was wondering what to ask. Then smiling, he asked me, "Where would. . . you boys. . . travel to?"

With the Mafnas Men resurfacing, I knew that he wanted to remind me to dream about it. "Japan?"

"Japan?" he nodded as he continued to dream with me. "Good choice."

I told him the things that we'd probably do, like go to Harajuku Street in the summer. I told him what I thought Matthew would do and how Dominic would stand out by just standing in the middle of the street.

The conversation went on until my dad shut his eyes. As I was about to leave the room, he said groggily, "Promise me. . . you guys will go."

His face was turned to me at the door, waiting for me to promise him. As fun as the idea seemed, I knew it would take a lot for us to travel. My mind raced to all the ways we could manage the trip until my dad pushed those thoughts away saying, "Stop thinking. And promise."

"I promise, Dad."

With that, he turned around with his back to me. "Thanks, son," he said.

I wanted to say that maybe when he got better, he'd be our tour guide. I didn't believe in all that jinx and super-stition stuff, but I just didn't want to risk it, so I kept my mouth shut about it. At that point, I'd do anything to keep the Man from jumping off our boat.

THE DAYS AFTER had my dad revert back to misery. It didn't take long until he reached a couple of days where he was still alive, but he was totally silent. No reaction, and if there was, it was incredibly small. My hopes that built up that one day were crashing hard.

I was washing the dishes, contemplating what I could possibly do to help him get to the state he was before, even though, deep down, I knew that it was impossible. I knew that that day was a good thing that happened in the midst of many bad ones.

"Veo!" I heard Auntie Connie's voice by the front screen door as she knocked on the metal. I washed off and let her in. "Where's Dominic and Matthew?" she asked as I kissed her cheek, but once I told her they were at work, I noticed the soft sad smile on her face.

"Where's your dad?" she asked like she always did, even though she knew he never moved.

"Same place," I pointed. She disappeared into his room.

I was too curious about what was up with Auntie Connie's mood that I tried to come into the bedroom only for her to tell me to leave her alone with Dad for a moment. She was in there for hours. I stood outside the door for a while, waiting, but it was too long that I sat on the couch. I fell asleep only to be woken up by Auntie Connie poking my arm with glossy eyes and puffy cheeks.

"Are you okay?" I asked. She nodded and pulled my arm as we walked outside and across the yard to her house. She was quiet until we were standing at her place.

"It's time." she said.

"Oh."

"I wanted to say goodbye."

I didn't believe her, and I wish I could remember the rest of that conversation, but it was mostly me consoling her. She wasn't calm anymore or concerned. She was only sad. But I refused to believe it, even though some part of me wanted him to let go of the pain.

Fuck. I said all the curses I'd ever known in my head after Auntie Connie disappeared in her house. I was growing angry because I didn't know what to hope for. I was so angry that I ran into the jungle just to yell and punch something. I punched and kicked so many trees that I still have scars on my knuckles to this day. But I remember once I broke down, I lay on the ground, sobbing, with the blur of the treetops blending green into the blue sky. It was a beautiful day, but a horrible one too.

I must have stayed there for a while because the only thing that told me to get up was the time telling me that my dad had to take his medicine. I got up, hating that I had to. I wished that I could freeze time to breathe and brace myself. But that wasn't an option. Aware that I was acting like a kid, I let myself pout, staring at each step that brought me closer to the house. But once I got to the steps leading to the screen door, I took a deep breath, regaining my composure. And like a responsible adult, I gave Dad his medicine before I helped him go back to sleep.

I went into the other bedroom, and stared out the window, taking in the smells of the moment, hoping to forget that my dad was dying. Maybe if there really was a god, he took pity on me, lulling me to sleep like my dad in the other room so I'd forget what I was going through, just for a moment.

My dad's last breath. I woke up at 2:17 a.m. I didn't know what woke me up, but to this day, I don't think it mattered because something was pulling me to the next room. My dad's room. I got up to find both Matthew and Dominic there. By the way their eyes and hair looked, it seemed like they just got up too. Nobody here minded how they looked, though. It was something we got from Dad. He taught us that unless there were visitors, our home was our oyster, our mess. I couldn't help but smile a little, knowing that he taught us well.

Matthew sat at the end of the bed with Dominic on Dad's right side. I planted myself on his left. We all seemed to know what was happening.

His eyes opened one last time. They were tired eyes, worthy of the rest that awaited them.

"Goodbye, Dad," Matthew said, rubbing his foot. Dominic hugged him and said, "I'll see you later, Dad."

His eyes were growing weaker. It was almost time. I wished there was more that I could give him just so he could ask me one more time how my day was. As I wished, I could only hold his left hand. "I love you, Dad," I said with a smile.

Maybe I imagined it, but I swear I saw a hint of a grin before his eyes shut.

It was his time, but I was aching for him to ask me one more time. Just one more. Just so I could tell him that my day was okay.

But he was already gone.

Epilogue

THE SOUND OF the disc scratching to a stop was noticeable. The memories were all floating in the air, fresh. It took a second to get back to the present, to remind myself to keep the disc that was my dad's, with his handwriting, filled with the songs that held our story.

Daniel's CD

Dominic was leaning against the couch. Matthew sat on the cushions with his chin and arms resting on top of the backrest. My brothers. There were things they didn't know, and for the sake of Dad's memory, they never would. There was no point in holding onto the negative parts of the past.

I felt myself smiling, wishing that he was still there. If he was, we'd be telling stories laughing about what happened then and at that time. But all we had at that point were songs, his old-fashioned playlist. There was something about songs that could shut a person up and feel moments as if they were the present. While I relived the memories associated with the lyrics and rhythms, I could hear the sounds of the hollow floor whenever someone walked on it, the screen door banging against the wood whenever someone let it loose instead of carefully putting it back in the lock, and the breeze blowing in, giving us all some temporary relief from the heat. Music. What a strange gateway to the past.

Knock. Knock.

Kayla came in. "Can I steal Matthew now?" she asked.

I grinned once I saw the look on Matthew's face pleading for help. "Sorry. I still need him here," I said.

"I'll be out soon, babe."

Kayla scanned our faces before nodding and closing the door behind her. I scrunched up my face, shooting a questioning look at Matthew.

"We always fight at weddings," he answered.

"She actually seems pleasant today," I said.

"Yeah. That's because she's hoping I propose to her soon. She keeps dropping hints, like 'Oh, we should just get married outdoors. More romantic' or 'Oh, they hired a great caterer here. We should get their number for ours!' or 'Oh my gosh, Matthew, you should totally have that hidden superhero photo done with you and your best men before the wedding!'" Matthew said before walking toward the exit door and pulling out a cigarette.

"That superhero thing sounds like something you'd want to do," Dominic said.

"It is, but I'm not taking the bait. Eventually, she starts asking the real questions."

"What are the real questions?"

Matthew puffed out smoke before answering. "'When are we getting married?' and 'Are we ever getting married?'"

"Well, are you?" I asked. "You've been with her for—"

"Yeah, yeah, yeah. I know. She just gets crazy at weddings."

Suddenly, a bang came from the door, and it opened. Kayla was standing there, fuming. Her lips drew back a snarl before her jaw clenched loud enough for us to hear across the room. But Dominic and I weren't normally scared of her, and today wasn't an exception. If anything, we felt like laughing at Matthew for getting caught. But we stopped ourselves in time as we looked at our brother who had straightened up and nervously put on a show.

"Babe, are you okay? We were just talking about how lovely you—"

"I get crazy at weddings? *I get crazy at weddings?*"

Now was the time to leave them. Dominic and I excused ourselves from the room as it stayed silent. It was almost time to be with Mia.

THE WEDDING HAD sand all over. A lot of it got into my eyes, resulting in awws from the crowd, since it looked like I was crying all the time. I heard Mia giggle whenever it happened too. "Sand in your eyes?" she mouthed as the minister continued. "Want to switch?" she mouthed again. But I only laughed and shook my head.

Matthew was still arguing where we'd left him. Everyone could hear it from the wedding venue, but it was okay. Everyone was already used to Matthew arguing with Kayla. If anything, it made me feel more like home, putting me at ease, especially since I didn't like being stared at by a bunch of people even if they were my family. But a brother fighting with his girlfriend? Such an odd antidote for being nervous in front of people.

Mia giggled again, bringing me back to the present. I wondered a lot if she could actually read minds, because she seemed to laugh whenever I thought of something worth laughing about. I always forgot to ask her about this possible quirk of hers, but I had all the time in the world to remember to ask her.

My cheeks started hurting, like a muscle that had been tense for a long time. I hadn't realized that I was smiling so much. I knew I looked like an idiot.

I forced my gaze away from Mia, and onto her parents sitting in the front. Her mom waved at me, worsening the ache in my cheeks. And her dad nodded my way, the same way my dad probably would have done if he were here today.

My eyes trailed off to my mom, who had an empty seat beside her. Somehow, I was hoping that my memories were all false and that my dad had just gone to the bathroom for a second. But my mom mouthed, "Uncle Nate," as she pointed at the seat.

I nodded back at her.

THE RECEPTION WAS overwhelming, so I found an escape to a balcony nearby. It was hidden behind the kind of curtains that nobody would bother touching or looking at a second time.

I took a deep breath in the warm night. The moon was large, larger than I had ever seen before. And it was a sight to enjoy.

"Veo?" I heard Mom's voice from behind. "What are you doing here?"

"Oh, uh, nothing," I started, before managing a smile to assure her that everything was okay. "What are you—"

"Oh, you're enjoying the moon, I see." She looked up at the night sky.

"Yeah," I chuckled.

"You know, I'll never forget that your first word was 'moon.' Why couldn't it be 'mama,' my boy?"

"I don't know, Mom."

"Yeah, well, I do." I looked at her, wondering what she thought the reason was, but there was no point in asking. "What's bothering you?" she asked.

"Nothing."

"You getting bored of being a manager? Always traveling for work?"

"Nonsense. I love it. It's a good job."

"Regretting getting married?"

"Not at all, Mom." I said as I shook my head, but she must have still detected something else was wrong.

"Is it because of your dad?"

I felt my smile disappear as I looked at her again. I took a deep breath. "Sort of."

"What is it then?"

I looked up at the sky, remembering that it was there, in that moment I had with Dad and Uncle Dun, even if the whole thing was something I imagined in my sleep. "I just had a dream of Dad last night. Him and Uncle Dun," I answered. Mom waited.

"We were talking about the wedding and Mia and Dominic and Matthew. It was a short dream."

"Sounds just like what your father would do."

"What does?"

"Visiting you in your dreams."

The crickets sounded louder as if they were trying to pull me to reality, the reality where science and rationality ruled over a god who made a world and saw that it was good, despite death happening for many plants and animals just to stay alive, which was supposed to be bad.

"It sounds like he visited you to wish you a good day, my boy." Her eyes gleamed at me. I pinched my nose at a thought that I considered ridiculous.

"Well, whatever you choose to believe, my Veo, I hope you're hoping that the last time you saw him isn't the last time you ever will." My mom patted my shoulder before telling me to come back to the party when I was ready. She kissed my cheeks and returned back to the food and dancing inside.

But before I returned my gaze to the moon, Mia came out. She was in her wedding dress that made her look like an elf from *The Lord of the Rings*. Only difference was that her hair was short like a pixie, just like she had it years ago. She had an unopened beer can in her hand as she smiled saying, "Your brothers want you to drink beer with them, my love." But she picked up on my vibe, asking me if I was okay.

"Yeah. No. My mom just told me this crazy idea that

my dad visited me last night," I chuckled, trying to lighten my mood.

"Oh? How'd he visit you?"

"A dream."

She gave a lopsided grin, tilting her head, waiting for me to go on.

"You already know I don't buy into the Christian thing, the Heaven and Hell thing. So it'd just be nuts to think that I'd be somewhere after I melt off this skin and these bones."

She hummed, thinking.

"What is it?" I asked.

"Well, what's wrong with hoping that they're right? Your mom and all the believers about the life after death?"

"Because you waste so much time in this life, hoping that your next one will be better even though you're unsure that you'll even get one."

"Isn't that the beauty of it though? Hoping that this isn't it? That you'll have much more time than how long your body tells you you're good for?"

I looked down. This wasn't the first time I had ever talked to her about these things, and she was always unsure about religion and all that spiritual stuff like me. But once I felt her hand on my cheek, bringing my eyes to meet hers, I knew that she was hoping that I'd see my dad again somehow.

She placed the beer can in my hand. It was the same brand of beer that my dad loved to drink. Bud Light. I locked her in an embrace, squeezing her until she squeaked. I wished that I had told Dad about her, that they had met before he left. But it was okay. I could hope that they would someday in another life.

When I let go of her, she grinned and said, "Well, whenever you're ready, my love." Then left the balcony.

Perhaps there was a Heaven or Hell like my parents believed, or maybe there wasn't. There was no evidence for it, but there was no harm in believing that spirits can visit. Maybe I'd meet him again in my next life. Who knew?

I opened the beer can and held it to the sky, about to repeat the words my dad used as a farewell, a good-bye without ever saying good-bye.

"Until then, Dad," I started, toasting to the moon. "May our times intertwine again."

M. P. REYES is the author of only one novel for now. As a homesick Chamorro/Filipino who originated from the CNMI, Reyes has an interest in writing that originated from a screenwriting class in college. Like many other millennials, she is still wondering what to do with her degree. But in the midst of all this confusion, she  is reflective of this short thing called life that ultimately inspires her stories.